TWISTED PULP
MAGAZINE

MAMMOTH MYSTERY

CLOSE TO MY HEART
By Chester S. Geier

JANUARY
25¢
IN CANADA 30¢

The SPIDER LILY

70,000 WORD NOVEL
BY BRUNO FISCHER

TABLE OF CONTENTS

- 4   Editorial
- 5   Interview with Craig Douglas of Close to the Bone Publishing
- 8   Spells, Unicorns, And The Old Ones A look back at Cast a Deadly Spell By Mark Slade
- 13   Iron Maiden: The Book of Souls Album Review By Kenneth Gallant
- 16   The Iceman Killeth By Andy Rausch
- 24   Femme Fatale Babes
- 30   Dick Powell Revisited: Chapter 1
- 39   Pin-up with Rita: Struggling with Pin-up and whether to continue
- 44   Interview with The Long Seventies Podcast
- 48   Pin-up: Rising Phoenix
- 54   Cosplay Corner with Amanda
- 57   Sermon Interrupted by Mark Slade
- 60   Pin-up: Katiya Rose
- 64   Dick Powell Revisited: Chapter 2

Photos by:
Katya Rose photos by Katya Rose
Rising Phoenix by Jukebox Beauties
Cherry Zette photos by Gaston
Lady Jane photos by Lady Jane
Rita Lazarus photos by Lily Soto

Doers of stuff:
Publisher Chauncey Haworth
Editor in Chief Lothar Tuppan
Assistant Editor Mark Slade
Resident artist Lavender Dragonfarm
IG@lavenderdragonfarm

EDITORIAL

A whole issue on Noir… who would have thought? One really needs to question what their goal is when publishing about a dead genre, like noir, and in a dead medium, like magazines. What am I doing? I like to think that I am creating art, or at least facilitating others to create art. But, does loving the past to the point of recreating it really count as art?

How much of art is about broadening the definition of art? We hear the idea often, that art needs to be fearless and push boundaries. Is that really what art needs to do, or was that just some super-high artist over-ruminating on the idea of being creative, that creativity must inherently be new.

Is holding on to a past genre indicative of a refusal to change or to grow beyond? I have wondered if we are just the publishing world's version of a cover band. Taking lines and melodies and rehashing them out in an ever so slightly different way.

My personal view of art is too self centered to try to break through walls. I'm not sure if I'm alone in this, but my creation process is more creating the same thing over and over in different ways until the time comes that I get it right… a time that never comes.

In a way humanity is doing this. A style transcends to become a genre, and a genre transcends to become an artform of its own. That art needs new torchbearers to champion the medium.

At least that's what I tell myself when I'm worried I'm wasting my time.

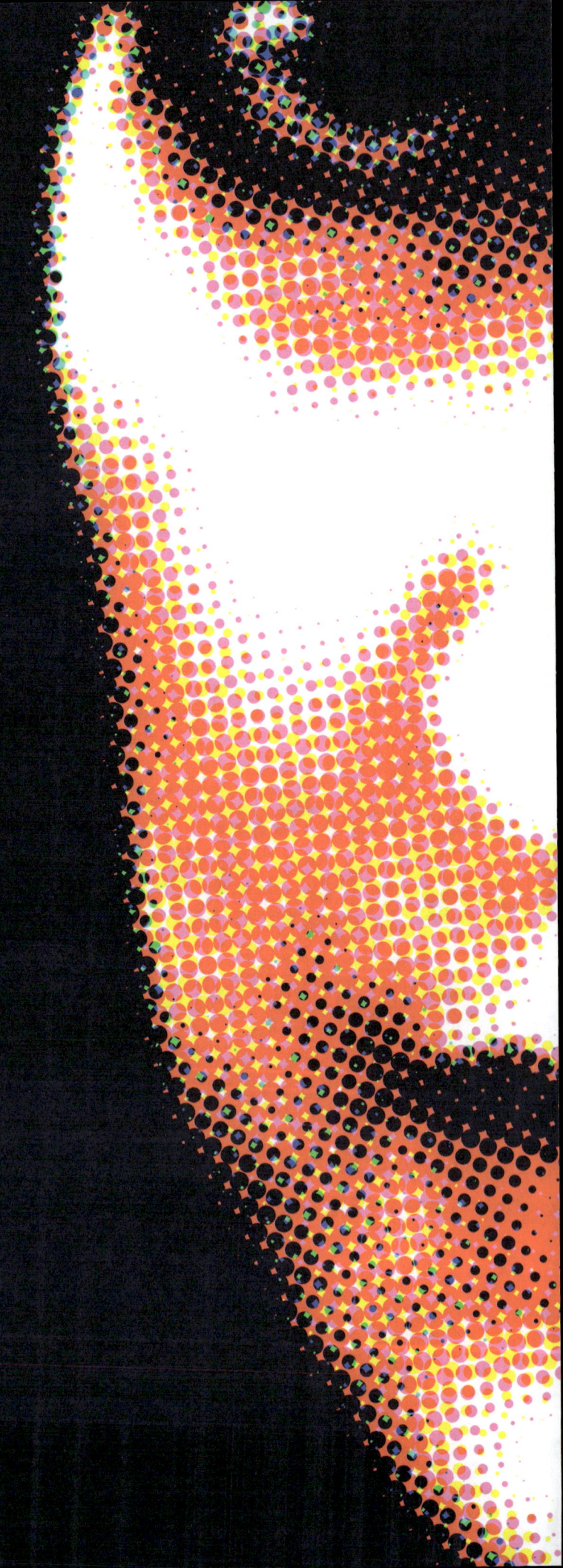

CRAIG
DOUGLAS
OF CLOSE TO THE
BONE PUBLISHING

Interview with Craig Douglas of Close to the Bone Publishing

Craig Douglas spent most of his youth traveling around Europe to various Forces locations as an Army Brat. He left school with no qualifications and joined the British regular Army as an Artillery Signaller. He completed 3 tours of Northern Ireland, Kosovo, Bosnia Herzegovina, Cyprus, Iraq and Afghanistan. A tour of Afghanistan sparked his urge to write and he kept a diary during his time there. FIRE MISSION : The Diary of a Firing Sergeant in Afghanistan can be found on Amazon, in both print and for Kindle. Craig is a Health & Safety Trainer/Consultant working in the UK and lives in the home of odd shaped footballs: Rugby.

Where are you from? What is your background?

I'm from a working class family, parents in the forces. I grew up in the north east of England and joined the British Army.

What inspired you to become a publisher?

I've loved writing as it's my creative awakening, it's how I can communicate, the medium of words are my love. I started publishing when Darren Sant decided to create an Anthology on the back of Close To The Bone short story website in 2013. We were already taking in short stories and this was the birth of my publishing experience. I found a knack of converting kindle books by using HTML and CSS and this evolved into paperback. When Darren left, I carried it on with a focus of getting fledgling authors onto the scene for them to be picked up by big publishers.

Why have you specialized in crime/mystery genre?

This was Darren Sant's idea. I'm not a fan of Crime/Mystery genre if the truth be told. It's certainly a genre widely used and it has scope to grow CTTB.

What advice do you have for writers who want to submit to your publishing?

Take advice, be humble and thank the person giving the advice as they've given up their time to read the work. Also, check the requirements for the manuscript. When they send a submission, they should send an introduction of themselves and attach the document as per the guidelines. Otherwise, it gets deleted or in the spam folder.

What writers and films were you into growing up?

I loved fantasy books, Fighting Fantasy, Dragonlance, Tolkien's works, Clive Barker, Stephen King. For films I was mainly into Bladerunner, Star Wars, Terminator, and Aliens.

Do you think your environment, where you live, has an effect on type of art you create?

It's mainly rural and I enjoy taking photographs of wildlife, sunsets, grungy places like ruins, rotting carcasses of vehicles. I remember reading a Clive Barker novel and getting a wonderful visual imagery of Liverpool and its terraced location.

What long term goals do you have?

To keep on helping authors out as much as possible. Perhaps I might even make a viable business out of this, have my own antique book shop…. I love books.

What do you think the popular culture will be like in ten years?

There'll be new trends, stuff that will seem alien to me and you probably. Each generation seems more alien, the more it subdivides and the older you get. Korean music, social media and the use of fast paced transport such as scooters, Bladerunner style taxis. I think the youth will be driven my the Mass Media and it has such a potential to sway public opinion and potentially weaponize large demographics of the global population for state actor's intentions.

What's the strangest thing you've been asked to do as a publisher?

Not sure there's been any strange thing, but working on someone else's website (which I will not do again). Provide a writer with 20 physical copies of their book, and £100 for the sheer delight of publishing their work.

What projects are you working on now?

Several crime novels, science fiction novels and a cross between Animal House and Animal Farm…. that's an interesting read. I'm also working on short story collections, the latest one from Mark Wilson.

CAST A DEADLY SPELL

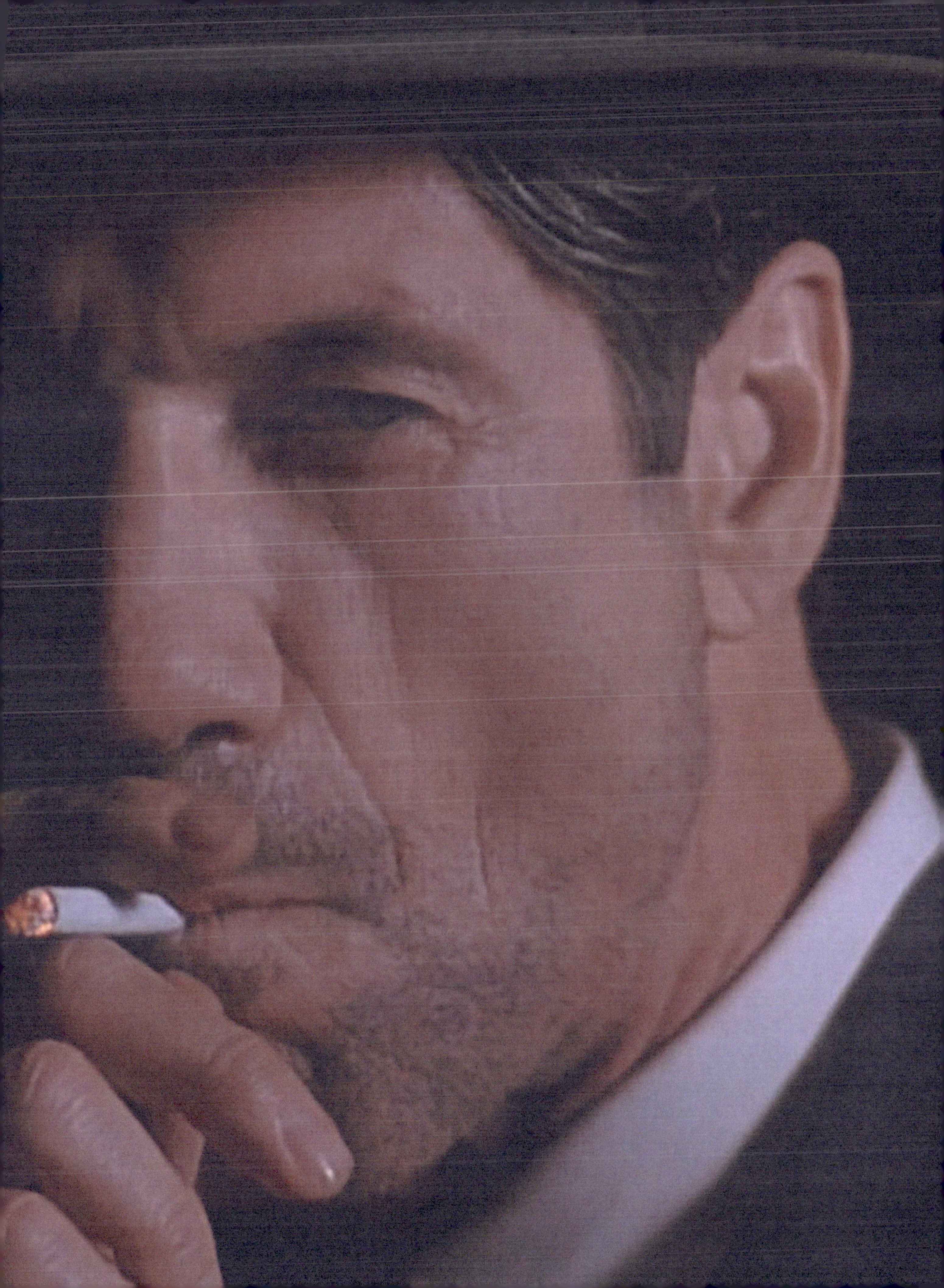

Spells, Unicorns, And The Old Ones

A look back at Cast a Deadly Spell

By Mark Slade

"They were going to have the whole world—have you heard of the old ones? The outsiders? Yog Sothoth? They're out there, Shamus. They've always been out there. Waiting for someone to unlock the door. It's in the book. Promise, power, price."

That's a quote from the underrated noir-horror film Cast A Deadly Spell (1991) starring Fred Ward, David Warner, Clancy Brown, and Julianne Moore (before she found fame in Boogie Nights and The Big Lebowski). HBO has done some great TV. Most recently True Detective and Boardwalk Empire. They have always been kind to genres in the past, especially Horror (The Hitchhiker and Tales from the Crypt). Cast A Deadly Spell is the perfect combination of Detective-noir and Horror as was Angel Heart. It definitely had just as good a cast.

In an alternate 1948 Los Angeles, Detective Phil Lovecraft (Fred ward—Remo Williams, The Right Stuff) is hired by rich business man Amos Hachshaw (David Warner—Time Bandits, Time After Time) to locate a book called the Necronomicon, which he needs the next day by midnight. Lovecraft is surrounded by folks who uses magic for everything, and employ Zombies to do their dirty work. In one scene we see a crew of Zombies trying build a house is insanely hilarious. The book has been stolen by a crony of Mafioso kingpin Harry Bordon (Clancy Brown—Highlander, the outstanding Buckaroo Banzai) but turns out the thieves double cross him. Lovecraft and Bordon go back, way back, to when they were L.A.'s finest. You see, Harry took bribes and Lovecraft didn't. Harry also uses magic, like everyone else, and Lovecraft doesn't, just on principle.

Lovecraft and Bordon have something else in common, lounge singer Connie Stone (Julianne Moore—Magnolia, Hannibal). Lovecraft and Connie used to share an apartment at one time. Turns out Hackshaw has been guarding his virgin stepdaughter closely for years. The stepdaughter, Olivia Hackshaw (Alexandra Powers—Dead Poets Society, Last Man Standing) has fun hinting unicorns with a bow and arrow while riding horseback. It's a ritual, as she says, giving grace to the Goddess Dianna.

There's more twists and dead bodies in this flick to make Dashiell Hammett give out a rebel yell from his grave.

One of the best characters is also my favorite in this film. Tugwell (Raymond O'Connor—The Rock, Drowning Mona) is a creepy little bastard, who loves to throw spells around like darts, and his victims usually find themselves a jacked up corpse.

There's more funny segments. Lovecraft traces a

suspect to a boarding house where the landlord is trying to repair his car. The landlord realizes the engine will not start because of Gremlins, and yes those pesky little creatures are in the style of Joe Dante's Gremlins. He opens up the hood of his 1930s vehicle, grabs a can of pesticide, he turns to Lovecraft and says, "When we went to Europe in WWI, all we brought back was the clap. They go off to WWII and bring back these little bastards!" Thusly spraying the giggling demonoids.

The idea that the whole world has turned to magic but one guy is poignant. It's a cry out for all of us to follow his or her own path, be a free spirit, don't be a sheep. And in a lot of ways, the references to Lovecraft and callbacks to the creatures and stories he created is also respectfully saying he was a free spirit. Lovecraft was, at least as a writer, never followed the current trend of his day. Maybe I'm looking too deep into an entertaining genre film. But those who are into the same kind of category as I am, will understand what I mean. Even though I have for the most part, out grown Lovecraft a little bit, it's great to see his work reach a Godly pantheon. I understand everyone's enthusiasm.

Not only is this a great cast with a great body of work behind them (and a future body of work) headlined by one of the very best character actors, Fred ward. I've seen films with him where he was not the star, but should have been. This movie shows that you don't need so-called A list stars to make it work.

Now the kicker. This was directed by Martin Campbell. Yeah, I know, the guy who pretty much killed off the Green Lantern franchise is burned in an effigy by Lantern fans every night. Before Green Lantern, Campbell was a respected New Zealand TV director, helming BBC classic, Edge of Darkness. He also brought James Bond back successfully, not only once (Goldeneye) but twice, (Casino Royale starring Daniel Craig). For that and this film, he should be respected… some.

There was a sequel in 1994 called Witch Hunt. It wasn't as good as Cast a deadly spell. It starred Dennis Hopper and it was kind of a waste of time and energy by both the creators and the audience.

From a little google search, I couldn't find a DVD release. I saw a link to the VHS. It's a shame, it deserves a blue ray and a look back documentary. That tends to happen, however rare nowadays, with some films.

KREATURE FEATURES

kreaturesandkreeps.com

BY BRACKETT

Album Review by Kenneth Gallant

IRON MAIDEN

THE BOOK OF SOULS

Iron Maiden: The Book of Souls

By Kenneth Gallant

The greatest band from the NWOBHM returns with their much anticipated 16th studio recording, proving the band can still create an epic sounding metal album. Of course I am talking about the one and only Iron Maiden and much news surround the band this time around. We recently learned of singer Bruce Dickinson's battle with cancer; surviving his ordeal and recuperating nicely at this point. Not to mention the recent news of embarking on another momentous world tour that will take them to 6 continents in a customized Boeing 747 piloted by none other than Bruce himself!

So how's that for a man who just went toe to toe with the dreaded disease and lived to sing another day! I think this proves that Maiden is all about being epic and let's face it—The Book of Souls runs the full gamut of life, death and tragedy! In other words, the album is a giant leap into a musical world that may astound the ears of many.

But what you get here is not the Maiden of old, so let's be perfectly clear about that. Sure there are glimpses of the classic era sound in a few of the tracks, but the bulk of it remains introspective and more on the progressive side. Now some fans may groan about the continual direction of the band and if you're not willing to sit through the 90 plus minute runtime, then you might as well give up now. But for those (like me) who adore this band, I suggest giving this new release plenty of attention, since its chalk full of magnificent moments—and plenty of variety to boot!

To start out with, lead single "The Speed of Light" is catchy as hell and ultimately sounds like an extension of "Can I Play with Madness" from 7th Son. I certainly felt it took me back to the late '80s and it might give disgruntled fans a chance to perk up their ears and take notice. I do however think the band made their first faux pas here by not allowing this to be the lead off track. Instead they chose "If Eternity Should Fail" as the opening number and it's a tad long and doesn't quite get the blood pumping as it probably should have for an opening number.

The familiar sounds of Steve Harris's flawless bass playing opens "The Great Unknown," signalling a return to '90s era Maiden in terms of pacing and tone. The track won't win over fans holding out for faster '80s material, but it does provide these ears with a bevy of harmonious sounds and tasteful riffs. Now the next track is the first of a handful of compositions that push the ten minute barrier and "The Red and the Black" is a song I really enjoyed. It certainly feels like a track that could have been on Brave New World (sounding a bit like "Wicker Man") and it never bores me nor does it feel like a strain on my ears; in an odd way I didn't want it to end.

The band picks up the pace on "When the River Runs Deep," getting back to a shorter and catchy little ditty that works for me. There's no qualm here though, especially since the moody opening of the title track "The Book of Souls" hits hard and forces the listener to pay close attention to the lyrics. Bruce displays some ominous sounding vocals and much of it reminds me of the material found on Brave New World and Dance of Death. The track is a lengthy one, but it really hits its stride around the six minute mark, making way for a meaty solo or two. This is a sure winner for me and I am looking forward to hearing this song in a live setting.

At this point we have digested about fifty six minutes of music and there's still another five tracks to get to! Again, this might be an exhausting listening experience to some, but for me I was spellbound to hear it all! In fact "Death or Glory" gets the blood pumping again, as does "Shadows of the Valley," which displays some morbid lyrical content ALA Dance of Death. If you are also wondering what references the band use here, just think about the biblical quotation psalm 23:4 and you will get my meaning. This is followed by another somber subject matter inspired for "Tears of a Clown," which is said to be about the death of Robin Williams. Not much more needs to be said about this number.

The remaining two tracks are a mixed bag for me. First let me say that "Man of Sorrows" is a downbeat mixture of "A Matter of Life and Death" and "The Final Frontier." Certainly not a bad track and obviously this has more in common with Maiden's current frame of mind as songwriters. This quickly gives way to probably the longest song Maiden has ever written and without question this is going to be the most controversial song with many fans too. Clocking in at almost twenty minutes in length, "Empire of the Clouds" is meant to be a sprawling epic, complete with orchestral arrangements and neoclassical metal approach—allowing Murray, Gers, and Smith to really stretch their progressive leanings. I think it might take the listener a few times to really get into this song, but you could compare this to "Rime of the Ancient Mariner" in some ways for sheer length and tonal qualities.

On a whole though, double albums can be a tricky affair, especially if the material lacks the inspirational spirt to carry them through. Book of Souls is not the case here and ultimately it will make Maiden fans run the gamut of many emotions, good or bad and definitely will continue to divide the camps wanting the classic era sound to return, and to those who enjoy the progressive approach to their song writing. I am firmly in the camp of the later and enjoy what the band is writing and can't wait to see this new beast unleashed on the next colossal tour.

THE ICEMAN KILLETH

BY ANDY RAUSCH

The Iceman Killeth

By Andy Rausch

October 8, 1981

"We know who you are, and we know what you do," the old man in the yarmulke said.

Richard Kuklinski, who would one day become known as "the Iceman," stared across the cement picnic table at him.

"Oh yeah?" Kuklinski said. "Who do you think I am?"

"We don't think, Mr. Kuklinski," the younger man, also wearing a yarmulke and sitting next to the old man, said, "We know."

"Okay, then tell me about it," Kuklinski said. "Tell me what you think you know."

Kuklinski looked absentmindedly at the children swinging on the swings and running and playing on the playground behind the two men. Then he looked back at the old man.

"You're a killer, Mr. Kuklinski," the old man said matter-of-factly.

"What is this? Fairy tale time?" Kuklinski said. "I'm leaving."

As Kuklinski flattened his palms against the top of the picnic table to push himself up, the younger man said, "We gave you $10,000 to take this meeting and hear what we have to say, so at least give us that."

Kuklinski remained tensed with his hands pressed against the tabletop, trying to read the faces of the two men across from him.

"There's more money if you accept our offer," the old man said.

This got Kuklinski's attention, and he relaxed some.

"I'm not saying I've done the things you think I've done," Kuklinski said, staring at them with a tough, no-bullshit stare, "but go ahead. You tell me what you came here to say. Then I'll let you know what I think. But first, tell me about the money."

The white-haired old man grinned. "Money wins out every time, doesn't it?"

Kuklinski just stared at him.

"We're willing to pay you $60,000," the younger man said.

Kuklinski raised an eyebrow. They had his full attention now. "Go on," he said, rubbing his bearded chin.

"You're a serial killer, Mr. Kuklinski," the old man said. "You've killed at least thirty people, and we're fairly certain that's just the tip of the iceberg. And you do what you do very well."

Kuklinski narrowed his eyes, and the two men saw fire in them.

"What makes you think any of that is true?" Kuklinski asked.

"It's not up for debate," the old man said. "We know."

"We know, and we don't care," the younger man added.

"Then what?" Kuklinski asked.

"We represent a group of very wealthy, very important people, Mr. Kuklinski," the old man said. "And we know a lot of things. Not just about you, but about other people too."

Kuklinski grinned a toothy grin. "Like what? What do you know?"

"Not only do we know that you are a serial killer who has also worked as a contract killer for the mafia, but we also know the location of two men who are hiding nearby who believe no one will ever know who and where they are," the younger man said.

Now grinning himself, the old man said, "But we know."

Kuklinski raised his eyebrow again as he eyeballed the

old man. "Who are these guys, and what do they have to do with me?"

"You generally dispatch your victims in extremely violent ways," the old man said. "Some of them you shoot, yes, but there have been others who were not so lucky. Others whose lives came to extremely brutal, savage ends."

Kuklinski held his palms out. "Whoa! Whoa! I've never killed anybody ever, not in my whole life."

Staring into Kuklinski's eyes, the old man said, "We're not here to get you into trouble. Again, we don't care. What you do or have done is of no concern to us, Mr. Kuklinski."

Kuklinski leaned in towards the old man. "Then what?"

"We wish to contract your services, Mr. Kuklinski," the younger man said.

Kuklinski gazed at the children playing behind the men again for a long moment. Then he looked back at the men, first the old man and then the younger one.

"Suppose I was the man you say I am," Kuklinski said. "I'm not saying I am, but just for shits and giggles, tell me about these services you're looking to contract."

The old man leveled his gaze at Kuklinski. "As you have likely surmised, Mr. Kuklinski, both my partner and I are Jewish."

The old man raised the left sleeve of his jacket to give Kuklinski a look at his forearm. When Kuklinski saw the numbers tattooed on the old man's paper-thin skin, he understood.

"You were in a concentration camp," Kuklinski said.

The old man looked at him grimly. "Auschwitz."

"I still don't understand what that has to do with me," Kuklinski said. "Lay it all out on the table."

The old man stared into his eyes. "As you might guess, Mr. Kuklinski, I am no fan of the men who committed these atrocities."

"Nazis," Kuklinski said.

"They took everything from me," the old man said. "They raped and murdered my wife. They shot my parents. They took away our children." There were tears in the old man's eyes, and he paused to compose himself. "What I am saying is, myself and many others—"

"The aforementioned wealthy individuals," the younger man said.

"We want very badly for these men to pay for the things they've done," the old man said.

Kuklinski stared at him. "I thought they hung 'em at Nuremberg."

"Not all of them, Mr. Kuklinski," the old man said. "Many escaped and went into hiding in different countries, using fake identities. Unlike the thousands of people they massacred, these men are still very much alive and free in the world, living their lives as if these things never happened."

"We cannot allow that," the younger man said.

"We will not allow that," the old man said sharply.

"Let me guess," Kuklinski said. "You've located some of them here in the states."

"We have located two of them, and they both live close by," the old man said. "Both men held prominent positions in the Third Reich."

"And they live here, in Jersey?" Kuklinski asked.

"No, they're both across the bridge," the younger man said.

"One of them lives in Queens, the other in Brooklyn," the old man said.

Kuklinski stared at the children playing for a moment as he considered this. He made a sucking sound with his teeth as he did. Then he looked at the old man. "So, why me?"

The old man grinned. "Who else would you send to murder such monsters? We don't just want them killed. We want them butchered the way they butchered our families. And that, Mr. Kuklinski, is your specialty."

Kuklinski nodded. "I'll do it. But I'll do it for $100,000. If you can pay me that, I'll do anything you want me to do to these fuckers, and I'll do it slow and painful."

"Exceedingly brutal?" asked the younger man.

Kuklinski flashed his big toothy smile again. "More brutal than your mind can comprehend. I'll paint the walls with their blood if that's what you want. I'll rip them to pieces."

The old man reached his bony hand across the table for Kuklinski to shake. Kuklinski didn't like to shake hands, but for $100,000, he could make the exception.

"How you dispatch them is up to you, so long as you make it very brutal," the old man said. "I cannot stress this enough. Also, we know you sometimes freeze your victims' bodies for long periods to obscure their times of death. This time, we would like you to leave their bodies behind so they will be discovered quickly."

"Why?" Kuklinski asked. "That's dangerous. It increases the chances of getting caught."

"We don't want you to get caught," the younger man said. "But we wish to make examples of these men."

"Yes," the old man said. "We want to frighten their comrades who also live in the States. We want them to know that justice—that vengeance—is coming. We want them to live in fear the way our families lived in fear."

Kuklinski winked at him. "For the amount you're paying, no problem."

oOo

Thomas Campbell, the seventy-one-year-old man once known as Colonel Werner Brinkmann, was sitting on his sofa watching the late show. It was a black-and-white picture about Martians fighting giant radioactive spiders. Campbell didn't care for such tripe and thought it beneath him, but he hadn't been able to sleep, and there was nothing better on.

There was no light inside Campbell's Brooklyn home beyond the minimal light provided by the television. On the screen, a green-skinned Martian was firing a laser pistol at a cheap-looking, obviously fake spider.

Campbell rolled his eyes at this and considered going back to bed, but knew he would not be able to sleep, so he would have to put up with aliens and spiders a bit longer. The television was positioned in the space between the living room and dining room, so he could see it from his sofa against the living room wall. As he was watching the movie, Campbell startled, his peripheral vision catching a movement in the darkness beyond the television. He squinted into the darkness, trying to make out whatever it was. He told himself it had just been his imagination, but, as it turned out, it had not.

He could see a human figure emerging from the darkness, slowly materializing in the dimmest of light. Campbell sat up upright but didn't rise to his feet. He put his hand up beside his eye as if it was a shield. There was a man there, just behind the television. A formidable-sized man, but Campbell could not make out his face.

"What do you want?" Campbell asked, startled by the volume of his voice.

"I'm here to make you pay," the intruder said.

"What do I have that I should pay for?!" Campbell asked.

The man laughed at this, simultaneously angering and frightening Campbell. He wished he had the pistol he kept beneath his pillow with him now. Then he could show this man, this... whatever. But as it was, Campbell did not have the pistol, and he knew he was neither quick enough nor steady enough to run past the man.

"Who are you, and what do you want?" Campbell asked.

His heart was pounding, and he found it difficult to breathe.

"I don't..." Campbell stammered. "I don't like this!"

The obscured man took a couple of steps towards him. He was now in front of the television, slightly to the left so the bright screen, which was suddenly blinding. Even though the man was closer now and Campbell could see his body, his face remained hidden.

"I'm sure people would think, 'How do you sleep at night, knowing how many men you've killed?'"

Kuklinski said, chuckling. "But you and I know differently. The deaths don't bother guys like us, do they, Werner?"

"Who are you?" Campbell asked again, not knowing what else to say. Then it occurred to him to reach for the lamp on his left and switch it on. He did this with his left hand, even though he was right-handed, so he wouldn't have to take his eyes away from the intruder. When the lamp came on, bright light flooded the room, and Campbell had to blink for a moment and then squint to see the intruder.

He was a tall, sturdy man. He was bald on top, with black hair visible on the sides of his head. He had a black beard with the tiniest bit of gray showing in it. Something was disturbing about the man, not just because he was standing in Campbell's living room clutching a butcher's knife. He would have been terrifying anyway. There was a coldness in his eyes and in his demeanor that gave Campbell chills.

Campbell stood, his skinny, weak legs trembling beneath him. "Please, no!" Campbell begged. Disgusted by the weakness in his voice, Campbell tried to compose himself. He stared into the man's eyes, frightening as they were, and said, "I can get you money. Is that what you want?"

Kuklinski grinned a sick, evil grin. "I don't want your money." He started coming towards Campbell now, and Campbell knew there was no way out. His eyes grew large, and when Kuklinski got close—he was right in front of him now!—Campbell tried to step back, his legs hitting the front of the sofa, causing him to fall back onto it.

Campbell put his palm up between them. "No! Please!" Kuklinski swiped the blade through the air—Campbell could hear it swoosh—and pain shot through his hand. Campbell instinctively looked down at his hand. When he did, Kuklinski grabbed his throat with his free hand and gripped hard, cutting off Campbell's air supply, and Campbell thought he was going to crush his larynx. Kuklinski raised him from the sofa by his throat. As Kuklinski pulled his hand back, Campbell found himself standing, and his eyes grew large. Before he could think or speak again, Kuklinski shoved him hard, and Campbell, trying to maintain his footing, crashed into the wall, his back and left shoulder taking the brunt of it. Campbell tried to stand erect again, but the man was on him before he could move, pressing him against the wall.

Kuklinski raised his hand and clutched Campbell's throat again, pressing his head hard against the wall. Campbell and Kuklinski were close now, staring into one another's eyes, and Campbell could smell garlic on the man's hot breath.

"You aren't so tough now, are you?" Kuklinski said.

Kuklinski then shoved the blade into Campbell's scrotum, causing him to scream in agony. Still holding Campbell up against the wall with his other hand, Kuklinski yanked the knife hard to the left, ripping Campbell's testicles. Campbell cried, screamed, and whimpered. Kuklinski dropped the blade so he could grab Campbell with both hands, and he flung his body down to the carpet like a rag doll. Campbell fell onto his side, his left arm pinned beneath him. Kuklinski stepped into the narrow space between the sofa and Campbell, then kicking Campbell as hard as he could, shattering several ribs as he did, onto his back.

Now that Campbell was lying on the floor, injured, weeping, and looking up at the ceiling, Kuklinski reached down and snatched up the knife from where it was lying beside Campbell's head. When Kuklinski stood erect again, towering over Campbell, Campbell stared up at him through bleary eyes. His lips were trembling, and he tried to speak, tried to beg Kuklinski not to hurt him anymore, but nothing came out except a whimpering moan. Kuklinski squatted beside Campbell, grinning as he did.

"How are you feeling, Werner?" Kuklinski asked. As Campbell stared at the face of death, even though his thoughts were racing and jumbled, one clear thought rose to the top—the intruder was a Polak.

"You... you are a Polack," Campbell mumbled. "I can't be killed by... a... Polack."

Smiling big, Kuklinski asked, "You don't think so?"

Campbell felt Kuklinski's blade push its way into his abdomen, just beneath his pajama top, and there was a sharp, excruciating pain unlike anything Kuklinski had ever felt before. He cried out again, calling for a god who either didn't exist or didn't give a shit about him. Kuklinski brought the knife up from Campbell's abdomen slowly, sawing, tearing his flesh, as well as every organ the blade came in contact with. As this was happening, the buttons of Campbell's pajama top popped loose one by one. He was screaming continuously now as the smiling Kuklinski was sawing his way through the thrashing Nazi's stomach all the way up to his chest.

Campbell was lying there, screaming and screaming—he couldn't stop—and Kuklinski pushed his hand down into Campbell's open abdomen, wrapping his fingers around a strand of his intestines. Campbell was still screaming, although his scream was dying out.

"Look at me, Werner," Kuklinski commanded. When Campbell didn't open his eyes, Kuklinski screamed the command. "Open your eyes, and you look at me, goddammit!" This did the trick and, despite the overwhelming pain Campbell was experiencing, he opened his tear-filled eyes. His screaming had transformed into a pained, pathetic wail now, and he saw Kuklinski gleefully pull his intestines out and hold a strand of them up before his eyes.

"It turns out you can be killed by a Polak after all," Kuklinski said, chuckling. He dropped the intestines now. Having murdered many people in a variety of ways, Kuklinski knew Campbell would be dead soon. The Nazi was weeping and moaning, his eyes clenched as tightly shut as he could manage, tears snaking their way down his cheeks.

"Hey Werner," Kuklinski said.

Campbell was oblivious to this.

"Werner, old buddy, you need to open your eyes and look at me one more time."

Campbell didn't seem to hear him, and Kuklinski concluded he had probably gone into shock. Nevertheless, the hopeful Kuklinski—hopeful that Campbell was not beyond the point of awareness—grabbed both sides of the man's head and plunged his thumbs deep into his eyeballs, feeling them pop beneath his nails like squished grapes. Whatever his mental state was, whether he was aware of what was happening or not, Campbell began to moan, making a sound like a dying pig, and his body began to thrash harder, and his arms flailed wildly. Still squatting over Campbell, Kuklinski wiped the blood from his thumbs on Campbell's open pajama top. Then he picked up the knife and raised it high over his head, plunging it down hard into Campbell's forehead with a loud crunch, and then, almost instantly, Campbell stopped moaning and thrashing. His body fell limp as if a switch had been flipped, shutting him off.

Kuklinski checked his watch. It was now three-ten. He'd have to finish up quickly if he was going to pay a visit to the second Nazi before sunrise. He would like to have waited and spaced the murders out, but it had to happen tonight because once the second Nazi learned of the first's murder, he would flee and find a new rock to hide beneath. So it had to be tonight. But that was fine because Richard Kuklinski was a man who loved his work.

oOo

Kuklinski rolled up to the park where he'd met with the two men previously. It was seven a.m. There were no children here, and the air was considerably cooler now. There was only one other vehicle in the park's small parking area, a Buick with the two men inside, waiting.

Kuklinski opened the car door and stepped out. Having seen him pull up, the two men had already gotten out and were making their way toward the Cadillac. Looking at them over the top of his car, Kuklinski said, "I took care of them. Did you bring the money?"

The younger man raised a briefcase over his head so Kuklinski could see it.

The younger man was ready to give him the money, but the old man was cautious. Coming around the back end of the Cadillac now, he asked, "How do we know you killed them?"

The younger man expected Kuklinski to take offense at this, so he was caught off guard when the killer smiled his big toothy smile at them. Kuklinski then leaned down into the still-open door of the Cadillac and grabbed the large duffel bag sitting in the passenger's seat. He pulled the bag out and turned toward them, tossing it onto the pavement.

The old man looked down at the bag. "What is this?"

"Take a look," the old man said to the younger man. From the expression on the younger man's face, it was clear that he didn't want to look in the bag. Still carrying the briefcase, he knelt and unzipped the bag. When he did, he remained motionless for a long moment, staring at the bag's contents.

Unable to see what his young partner was seeing, the old man asked, "So, what do you see?"

Immediately, as if responding to the question, the younger man turned and spewed vomit onto the pavement. A moment later, embarrassed, he wiped his mouth with his sleeve and stood.

Kuklinski grinned proudly.

"It's that bad?" the old man asked, a hint of glee creeping into his voice.

"Heads," said the younger man. "Heads without eyes."

The old man nodded. "Give him the money."

The younger man held out the briefcase for Kuklinski. Without saying a word, Kuklinski took the briefcase, smiled at them one last time, climbed into his Cadillac, and drove away.

oOo

STORY NOTES FOR "THE ICEMAN KILLETH": For those who aren't aware, Richard Kuklinski, a.k.a. "The Iceman" was a real serial killer. Because Kuklinski claimed to have killed more than 100 people and also worked as a mafia hitman, I've always been fascinated by him. This story is an odd mixture of themes I was interested in, and I had a good time writing it.

TONS OF AWESOME TWISTED PULP MAGAZINE ISSUES AVAILABLE!

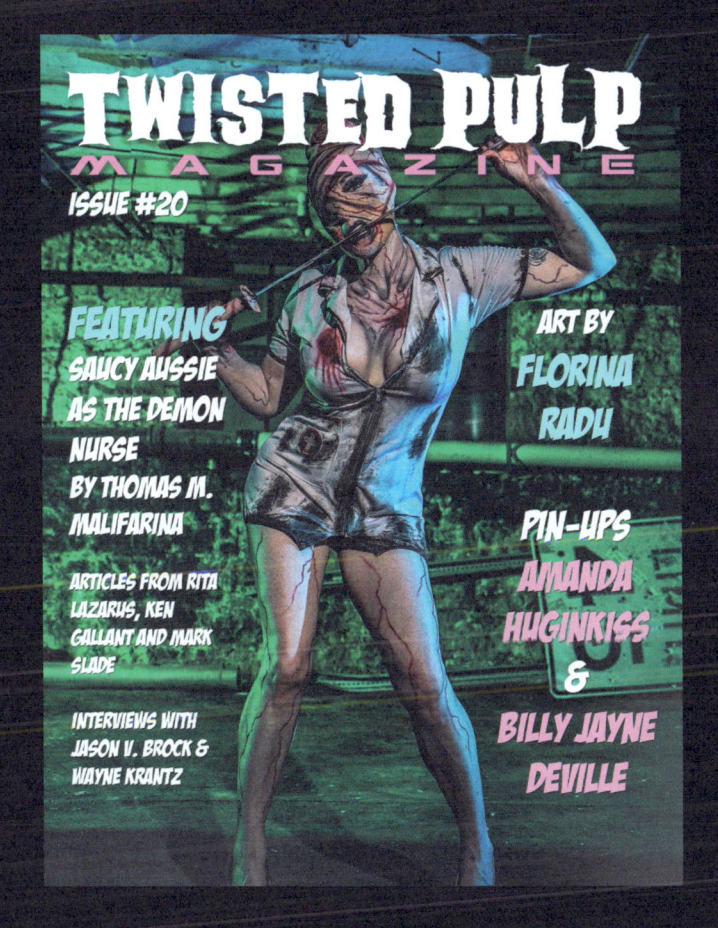

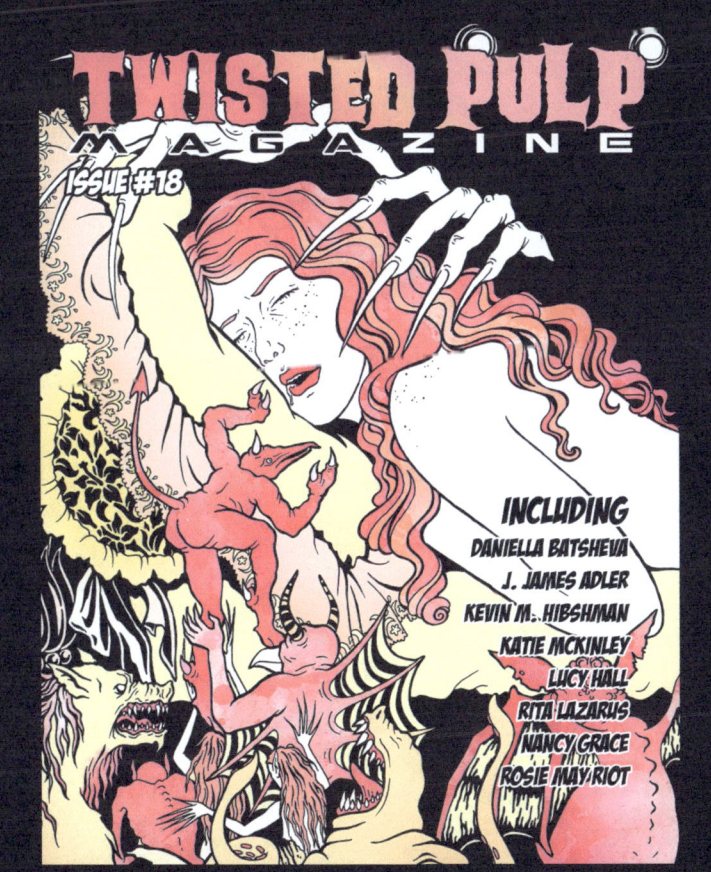

TWISTED PULP MAGAZINE — ISSUE #21

FEATURED INTERVIEWS

DANNY STEWART & MEREDITH LAXTON

INCLUDING STORIES FROM MARK SLADE & MATT LENNOX

PIN-UPS!
RITA LAZARUS
SPOOKY SUSIE
THE MARY LUST
LADY DEVINE

TWISTED PULP MAGAZINE — ISSUE #20

FEATURING SAUCY AUSSIE AS THE DEMON NURSE BY THOMAS M. MALIFARINA

ART BY FLORINA RADU

ARTICLES FROM RITA LAZARUS, KEN GALLANT AND MARK SLADE

INTERVIEWS WITH JASON V. BROCK & WAYNE KRANTZ

PIN-UPS
AMANDA HUGINKISS & BILLY JAYNE DEVILLE

TWISTED PULP MAGAZINE — ISSUE #19

FEATURING
LAVENDER DRAGONFARM
L.K. INGINO
KEVIN QUIGLEY
MICHAEL GOLDBERG
CHERRY ST
JAZMIN FORREST

WITH PIN-UPS
RITA LAZARUS
MISS SCARLET BLAZE
MISS SATINE LEMANS

TWISTED PULP MAGAZINE — ISSUE #18

INCLUDING
DANIELLA BATSHEVA
J. JAMES ADLER
KEVIN M. HIBSHMAN
KATIE MCKINLEY
LUCY HALL
RITA LAZARUS
NANCY GRACE
ROSIE MAY RIOT

femme fatale (*plural* **femmes fatales** *or* **femme fatales**)
1. An attractive and seductive but ultimately dangerous woman.

FEMME
FATALE
BABES

babes
1. *plural of* **babe**
2. (*treated as a singular noun; plural* **babes**) Alternative form of **babe** used as a term of endearment to a loved one.

OH, MY OFFICER, MY SUSPENDER HAS COME UNDONE. CAN YOU HELP ME WITH THAT

YOU REALLY THINK I AM CAPABLE OF MURDER, OFFICER?
YOU CAN CHECK MY SHOES FOR BLOOD, IF YOU LIKE.
I'M REALLY NOT A BAD GIRL, OFFICER. UNLESS YOU WANT ME TO BE...
WHY HELLO, OFFICER. YOU CAUGHT ME AT A... BAD TIME.

HMMM.....I COULD INHERIT HIS FORTUNE.

HELLO, POLICE, MY POOR HUSBAND JUST DIED OF A HEART ATTACK, SNIFF!

HUBBY IS GONE, WHY DON'T STAY AND HAVE SOME FUN WITH ME?

OH HELLO NEIGHBOR. NEVERMIND HOW I GOT IN, LET'S HAVE SOME FUN.

LEAVE ?! DARLING, I'LL NEVER LEAVE YOU!

KREATURE FEATURES BY BRACKETT

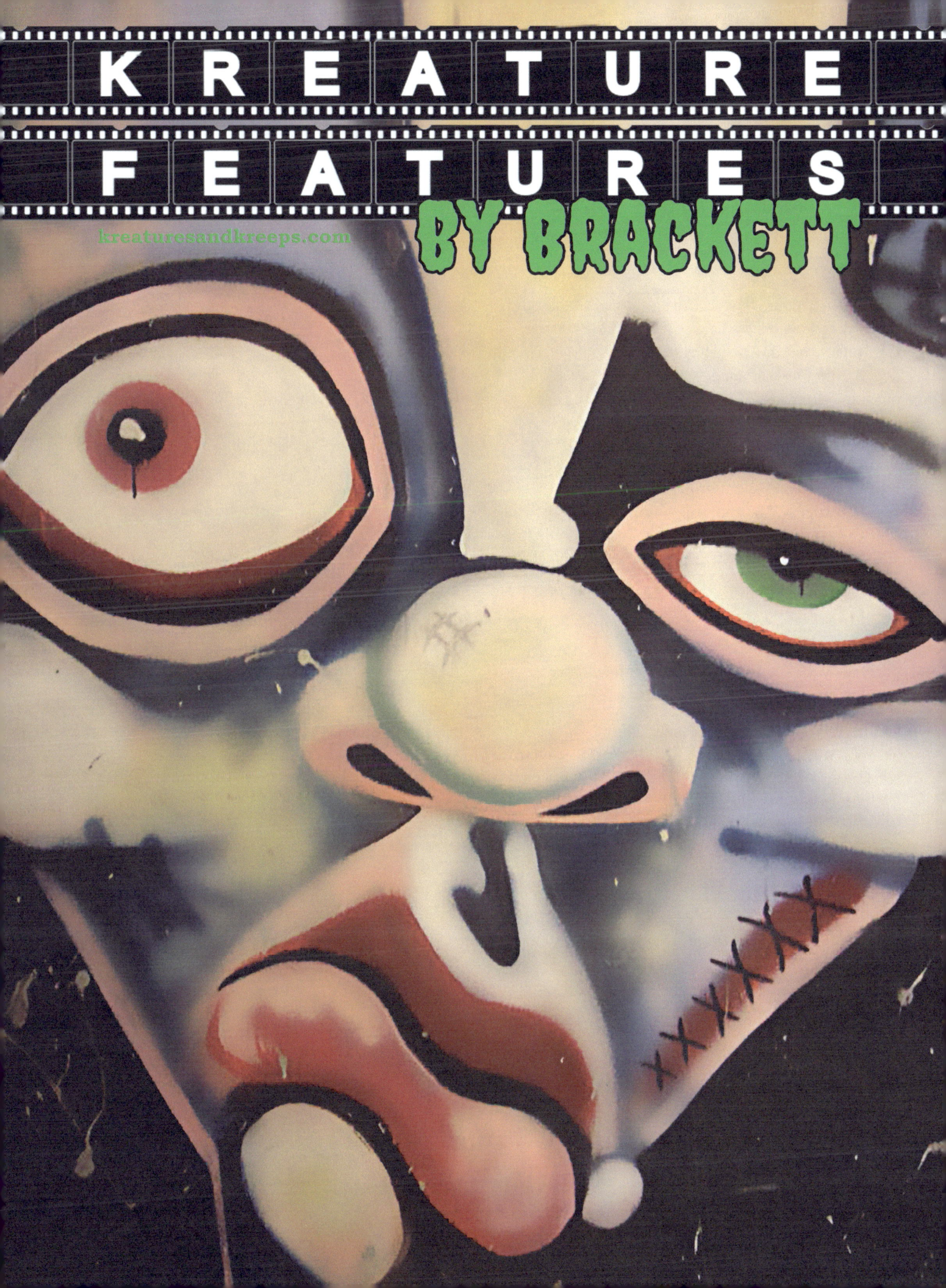

kreaturesandkreeps.com

Dick Powell

Dick Powell came to stardom as a musical comedy performer with his first big role in 1932 's Blessed Event. He went on to play more comedic roles until he decided that he had aged out of comedy and started pursuing more adult, "tough guy" roles.

Powell was the first to play hardboiled detective Philip Marlowe on the screen. He stared in a series of 11 movies based on Raymond Chandler's novels. The first one, "Murder My Sweet," was nominated for an Oscar. The series was so popular that it spawned a radio show and comic books, as well as an NBC television series called "Philip Marlowe."

In 1962 Powell acknowledged rumors that he was undergoing treatment for cancer, which had been previously diagnosed as allergies. It is speculated that he developed cancer due to the film The Conqueror (1956), which was filmed at St. George, Utah, near a site used for nuclear testing. Almost a third of the actors who participated in the film developed cancer, including John Wayne, Susan Hayward and Agnes Moorehead.

Powell's last movie as Marlowe was "The Long Goodbye" (1973), which was released after his death.

DICK POWELL in "FIVE FINGERS OF SATAN"

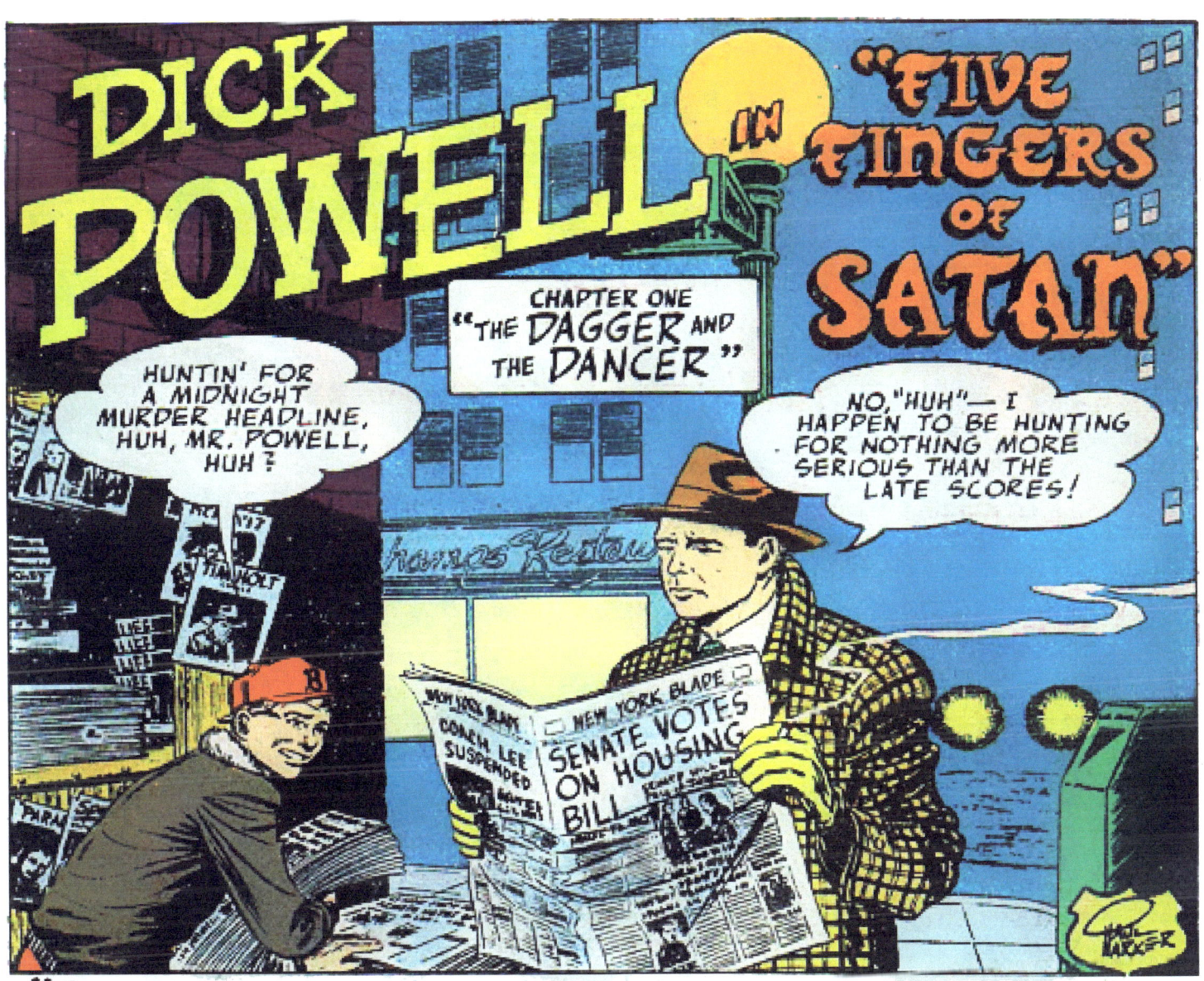

CHAPTER ONE "THE DAGGER AND THE DANCER"

"HUNTIN' FOR A MIDNIGHT MURDER HEADLINE, HUH, MR. POWELL, HUH?"

"NO, 'HUH'— I HAPPEN TO BE HUNTING FOR NOTHING MORE SERIOUS THAN THE LATE SCORES!"

"JUST RELAXING, EH, MR. POWELL?—THE LATE PAPERS, PERHAPS A CUP OF COFFEE, A FEW PLEASANT DAY DREAMS AND A BLEEDING BODY! WHERE DID THE CORPSE COME FROM? WHY, FROM THAT LIMOUSINE JUST A LITTLE WAY DOWN THE STREET!"

"TH-THIS IS INSANE... A NIGHTMARE! I'LL NOT SIT HERE AND BE HERDED OFF LIKE A STEER TO ITS SLAUGHTER!"

"OPEN THE DOOR! I-I CAN'T HOLD HIM ANY LONGER!"

"RIGHT!"

"VERY WELL, MURAT—TAKE YOUR FREEDOM... AND THIS 'FORGET-ME-NOT' WITH IT!"

SCREEEEECH

I— I'VE BEEN...
YEAH, I KNOW PAL..."I'VE BEEN AT A PARTY THAT PROVED JUST A LITTLE TOO SPIRITED!"
UH-UH, POWELL —HOLD TIGHT!
H-HELP ME... UHHHHH!
SOMEBODY YA KNOW, HUH, MR. POWELL? HE SICK OR SOME-THIN', HUH?
YEAH...RUN AROUND THE CORNER AND GET A COP, WILL YOU, KID!
MURAT! JAN MURAT ...CAN YOU HEAR ME?
H-HEAR YOU... T-TAKE THIS...
KNOW HIM?
SORT OF! READ PLENTY OF HIS BOOKS AND... HOLD IT— HE'S TRYING TO TALK!
CONSULATE ...VANIDA...THE FIVE FINGERS OF SATAN...AAHHHH...
I DON'T GET IT! HE DIDN'T FINISH...
I'M AFRAID HE IS FINISHED, FRIEND!
LATER, IN HIS ARGYLE ARMS APARTMENT, AS POWELL TOYS WITH THE RABBIT'S FOOT...
UH-UH! THOUGHT THERE MIGHT BE MORE TO THIS HARE'S HIND LEG THAN A LOAD OF BAD LUCK...A KEY, TUCKED IN THE TUFT OF FUR!
2

BETTER PLAY ON THE LEVEL WITH THE LAW AND TURN THAT KEY IN FIRST THING TOMORROW!
AND, AS THE MANTLE OF MORNING MIST LIFTS FROM THE CITY...
HOW'S IT GOING, KID?
NOT SO GOOD! THAT ACCIDENT WE SAW SORTA GAVE ME NIGHT-MARES!
ACCIDENT?!
YEAH, THAT MURAT GUY! THE STORY'S ON PAGE FOUR!
NEW YORK BLADE
YANKS SET FOR FIRST
HMPH! THIS PIECE IS PHONIER THAN A CARNIVAL CHANCE WHEEL!
JAN MURAT ACCIDENT VICTIM
SEE, IT'S LIKE I TOLD YOU, HUH?
YEAH... JUST LIKE YOU TOLD ME, KID! SEE YOU LATER...
NOW I'M GOING TO TELL ONE—TO THE COPS!
I TELL YOU THAT KNIFE STOOD OUT OF MURAT'S BACK AS PLAIN AS THE NOSE ON YOUR FACE, INSPECTOR! AND WHAT ABOUT THAT FARE-WELL PHRASE MURAT MUMBLED?
WELL—WHAT ABOUT IT?
LOOK! HAS THE WHOLE DEPARTMENT SUDDENLY GONE DEAF, DUMB AND BLIND?
EXACTLY, POWELL, AND I'D ADVISE YOU TO BECOME SIMILARLY AFFLICTED! THIS AFFAIR IS STRICTLY "HANDS OFF!"
3

LET'S GET THINGS STRAIGHT, POWELL... MURAT'S MURDER IS A HOT INTERNATIONAL POTATO THAT NEEDS GOVERNMENT HANDLING! AND I'M SURE THAT UNCLE SAM CAN DISPENSE WITH YOUR SERVICES!
IN OTHER WORDS —"HERE'S YOUR HAT!" OKAY, VELTMAN, YOU'RE THE DOCTOR!
AFTER THE BRUSH-OFF I GOT THERE'S NO NEED RUSHING TO TURN THAT KEY IN!
NO PARKING POLICE DEPT.
HEADIN' UPTOWN, MR. POWELL?
YEAH, MAXIE... FERRY ME UP TO SUTTON AVENUE! I'VE GOT A KEY THAT WANTS TO SEE A DOOR ABOUT A FITTING!
CHECK!
MINUTES LATER, IN FRONT OF MURAT'S MIDTOWN APARTMENT...
STICK AROUND, MAXIE! BE BACK IN A MINUTE!
FITS!
NOW THE TRICK IS TO TIE UP MURAT'S LAST WORDS WITH THOSE PILES OF PAPER ON HIS DESK!
YE-AH—THIS MIGHT BE IT... "THINK OF A HAND, SPREAD OUT AND MENACING. THINK OF THE FIVE FINGERS..."
4

WHAT WAS IT THAT MURAT SAID... "THE FIVE FINGERS OF"...
THE FIVE FINGERS OF SATAN, MY FRIEND! NOW, THE PAPER, PLEASE!
THANK YOU! IT IS MOST UNFORTUNATE THAT I MUST REPAY YOU FOR YOUR COOPERATION WITH...
NOW, WHAT THE...
...THIS!
SORRY, BEAUTIFUL, BUT YOU'LL HAVE TO BURY THAT BLADE ELSEWHERE!
LET'S LEAVE IT IN THE DESK, EH, BABE!
HIT HIM AGAIN, LATHAM... AGAIN!
GLADLY, VANIDA!
BEFORE POWELL'S BLURRING EYES HIS TORMENTOR TAKES ON THE APPEARANCE OF A BLACK DISSOLVING MASS...
...INTO WHICH POWELL IS PULLED AND PLUMMETED DOWN THE BOTTOMLESS WELL OF UNCONSCIOUSNESS!
5

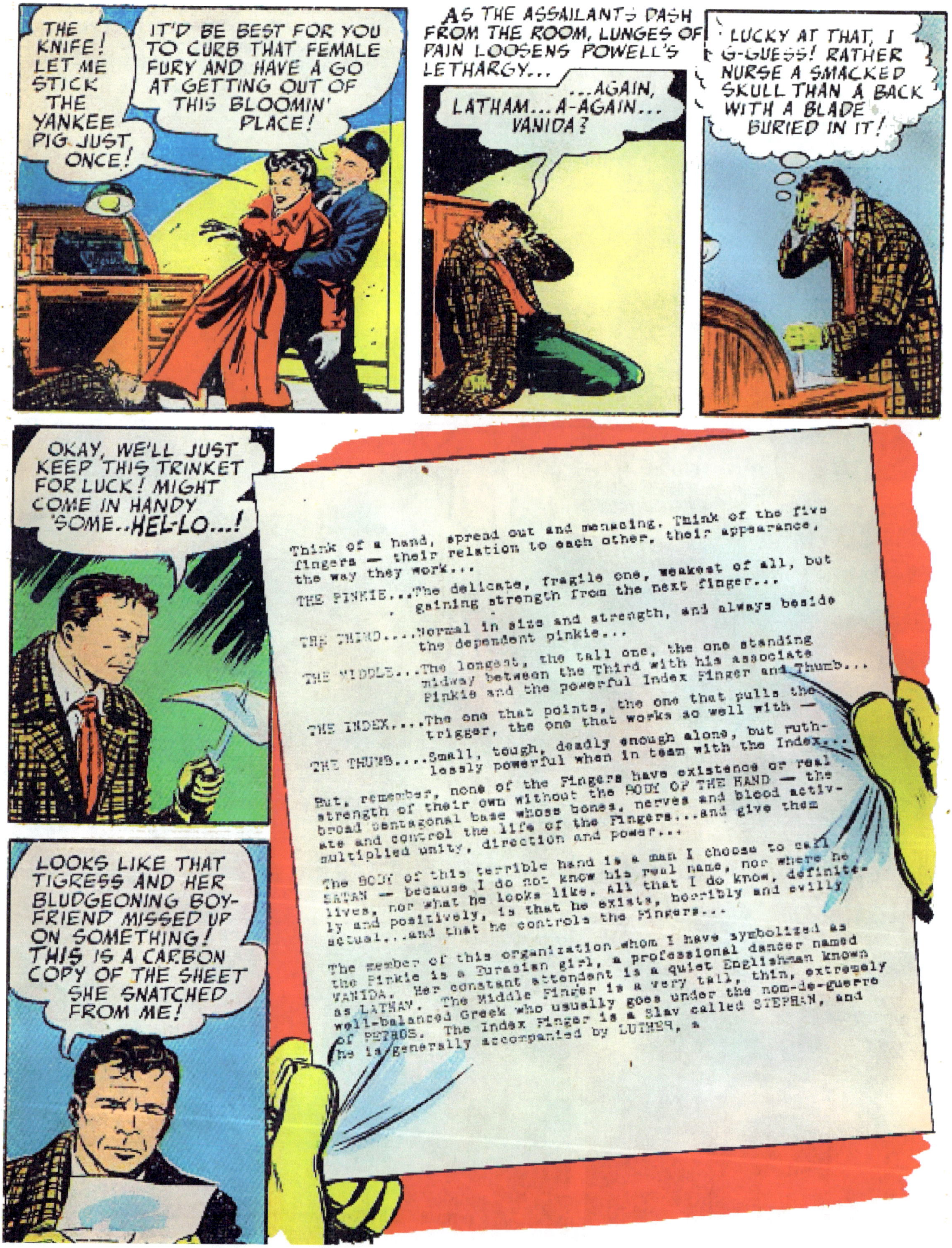
THE KNIFE! LET ME STICK THE YANKEE PIG JUST ONCE!
IT'D BE BEST FOR YOU TO CURB THAT FEMALE FURY AND HAVE A GO AT GETTING OUT OF THIS BLOOMIN' PLACE!
AS THE ASSAILANTS DASH FROM THE ROOM, LUNGES OF PAIN LOOSENS POWELL'S LETHARGY...
...AGAIN, LATHAM...A-AGAIN... VANIDA?
LUCKY AT THAT, I G-GUESS! RATHER NURSE A SMACKED SKULL THAN A BACK WITH A BLADE BURIED IN IT!
OKAY, WE'LL JUST KEEP THIS TRINKET FOR LUCK! MIGHT COME IN HANDY SOME..HEL-LO...!
LOOKS LIKE THAT TIGRESS AND HER BLUDGEONING BOY-FRIEND MISSED UP ON SOMETHING! THIS IS A CARBON COPY OF THE SHEET SHE SNATCHED FROM ME!
Think of a hand, spread out and menacing. Think of the five
fingers — their relation to each other, their appearance,
the way they work...
THE PINKIE...The delicate, fragile one, weakest of all, but
gaining strength from the next finger...
THE THIRD....Normal in size and strength, and always beside
the dependent pinkie...
THE MIDDLE...The longest, the tall one, the one standing
midway between the Third with his associate
Pinkie and the powerful Index Finger and Thumb...
THE INDEX....The one that points, the one that pulls the
trigger, the one that works so well with —
THE THUMB....Small, tough, deadly enough alone, but ruth-
lessly powerful when in team with the Index...
But, remember, none of the Fingers have existence or real
strength of their own without the BODY OF THE HAND — the
broad pentagonal base whose bones, nerves and blood activate and control the life of the Fingers...and give them
multiplied unity, direction and power...
The BODY of this terrible hand is a man I choose to call
SATAN — because I do not know his real name, nor where he
lives, nor what he looks like. All that I do know, definitely and positively, is that he exists, horribly and evilly
actual...and that he controls the Fingers...
The member of this organization whom I have symbolized as
the Pinkie is a Eurasian girl, a professional dancer named
VANIDA. Her constant attendant is a quiet Englishman known
as LATHAM. The Middle Finger is a very tall, thin, extremely
well-balanced Greek who usually goes under the nom-de-guerre
of PETROS. The Index Finger is a Slav called STEPHAN, and
he is generally accompanied by LUTHER, a

37

HEY, WAIT A SEC, MR. POWELL ...IT'S LOOEY! IT'S LOOEY!
YOU'RE LATE, LOOEY! WHERE WAS YOU!
I GOT STUCK WITH A BRUNETTE AND A LIMEY ON A RUN OUT TO THE AIRPORT!
YER DOIN' FINE, LOOEY! KIN YOU REMEMBER THEM SAYIN' WHERE THEY WAS HEADIN' FOR?
ER... YUP... LISBON, PORTU-AH-PORTUGOOSE!
THAT'S IT, MAXIE! LET'S GO!
VIA MAXIE'S TAXI, POWELL RACES TO THE MUNICIPAL AIRPORT AND...
NEXT FLIGHT TO LISBON AT 10:35 P.M., SIR!
OKAY, HON...GIVE ME A ONE-WAY TICKET!
DAWN FINDS DICK AIRBORNE OVER THE ATLANTIC AZORES— TOWARD THE PORTUGUESE PORT...
MEANWHILE, IN ONE OF LISBON'S MORE LURID LITTLE CAFE CENTERS...
HAH— THEES POSTER WEEL DRAW OOGLING FOREIGNERS LAK FLIES! THEY WEEL PAY MUCH ESCUDOS TO SEE THEES BEAUTY!
Cafe Estrella
CAFE ESTRELLA PRESENTS
VANIDA
CONTINENTAL SWEETHEART!
DANCING HER FAMED FLAMENCO TONIGHT
8

Pin-up With RITA!

Pin-up with Rita

All photos by Lilly Soto of Perfectly Pinup

Struggling with Pin-up and whether to continue

Everyone talks about the positives of pin-up because well, there are a lot of them. But people don't talk about negative things or if they struggled with things in the community.

I first got into pin-up about 9 years ago and I was bright eyed, excited, enthusiastic, and dressed up every day. And let me tell you it is a lot of work to get dressed up like that every day; curl the hair, apply the make-up, your outfit, your undergarments, your shoes and jewelry and even a purse, gloves, and possibly a hat or hair flower. And while you look and feel beautiful and amazing – you get asked lots of stupid questions. "Why are you wearing a costume; Are you in a play? What are you all dressed up for?" And I would smile and say, "I'm dressed up for life honey, you should try it." Of course, there were also nice people that would just be nice and give you compliments and well none of it really matters because we dress for ourselves not anyone else. I also remember when I would come home from work or being out and while being dressed up is fun it is also tiring. First thing I did when I came home is "unpin" myself—and be in pajamas and no make-up. Ah…. now I can relax.

I became so immersed in it that I was at car shows every weekend, doing pin-up competitions, and doing photo shoots and submitting to pin-up magazines and getting in those magazines. (Side note – as a pin-up you are your own advocate; you pay for your photo-shoots, hair and make-up, clothes, accessories, and you submit to the magazines—a time consuming and an expensive hobby. But I was so proud of myself for doing far more with pin up that I ever intended to. And you see when I first started going to car shows I did not know anyone so I would go by myself and not everyone was so friendly. l Eventually I made friends and that is another thing about pin-up—you get to meet so many cool like-minded people.

When Covid hit and we were all working from home—there was no reason to dress up anymore. Plus before becoming a pin-up, I was Goth and still am. That part will never leave me. As the saying goes If Persephone can be Queen o f the Underworld and Goddess of the Spring, so can we. I tried a few times to dress pin-up, but it was a lot of effort to sit around my house. And even before this I struggled with do, I even want to be a pin-up anymore? I am a very observant person and I started to notice things, things I did not like, started to see things that I did not think were fair and I know "life is not fair."

Going to Viva East this past year was a lot of fun and changing outfits several times a day made me realize how much I missed getting dressed up and I got to meet so many amazing people. When I got back home that feeling sort of went away, I guess you could say, and I started thinking maybe I shouldn't do this anymore. I am lucky to have so many supportive and encouraging people telling me not to stop; that I am so good at it. That maybe I shouldn't worry so much about pin-up contests and just dress up for me. To be honest, I still don't know. I think to myself: it's just easier to just wear all black.

Here's the thing, we are creators of our own truth, of our own destiny, of our own fate. It's ok to not be a pin-up 24/7 – that doesn't make you any less of a pin-up. And its ok if you want to take a break and step back. It's all ok. We have this one life. Be happy. Find what brings YOU joy. Dress for you and love yourself. And I will say this – I never thought I would be a monthly pin-up columnist for a magazine and that is something that brings me joy. Just be you.

Love,

Rita XOXO

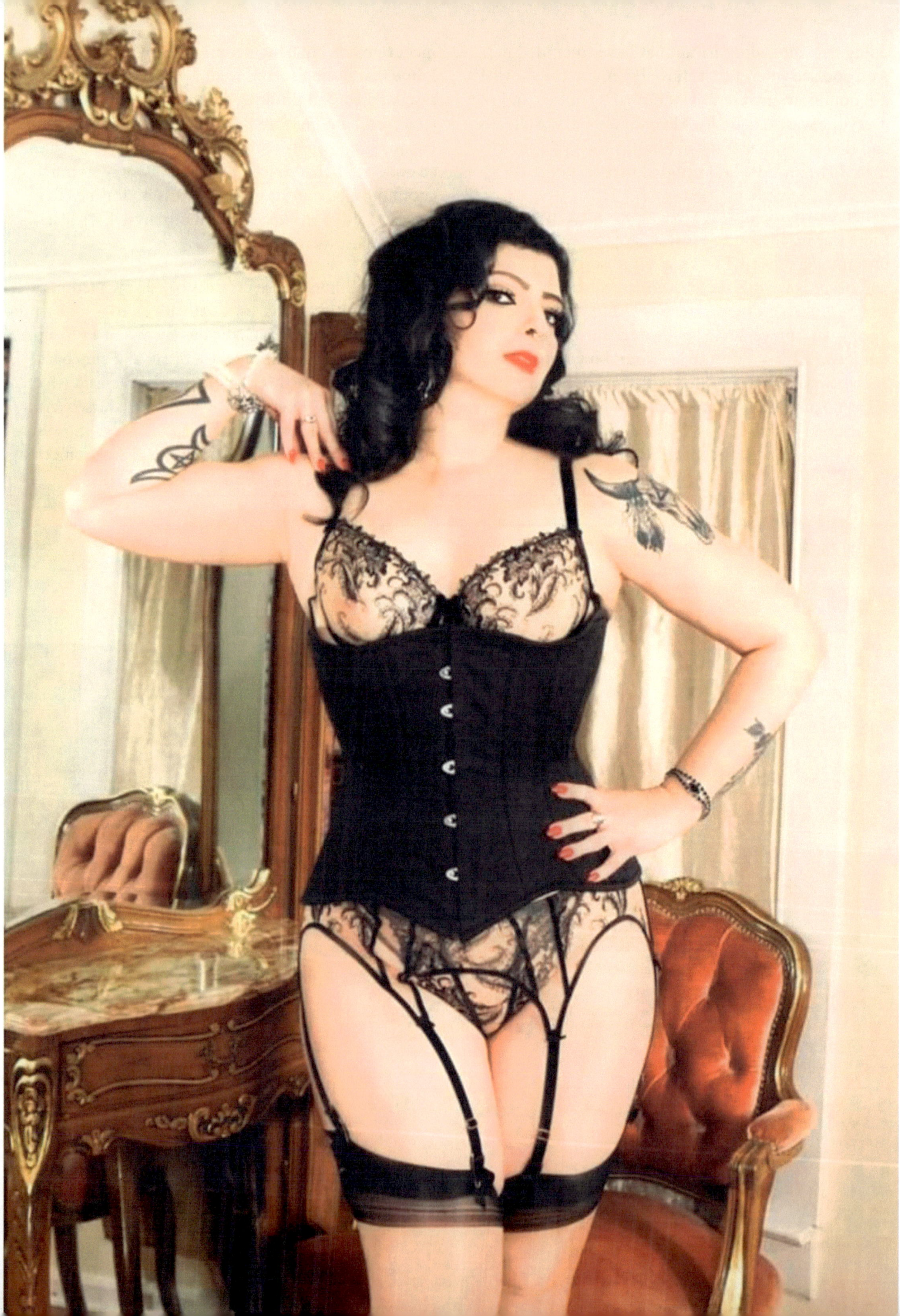

KREATURE FEATURES BY BRACKETT

kreaturesandkreeps.com

BRACKETT

INTERVIEW WITH

The Long Seventies Podcast

The Long Seventies Podcast is an in depth historical exploration of all things 1970's, including politics, film, television, literature, music, culture, science and artistic/philosophical movements

Where are you from? What is your background?

Matt: I am a midwesterner transplanted to Silicon Valley as a child, which explains why I can empathize with being drafted to fight in Vietnam so well.

Alex: Midwest, West Coast, and Midwest again. Worked in libraries the most.

What inspired you to do podcasting, specifically about the 1970s.

Matt: I was a History major in college and the only history class that ever explored the post WWII period was focused on the 1970s. The primary text we used was a book called The Seventies, by Bruce J. Schulman. This book introduced the concept of the Long Seventies and was, for me, a new way of looking at history as a set of trends and metatrends that defined a period more than a decade. This was not an entirely new concept, but Schulman's argument defined the period so well that it stuck with me and eventually became the inspiration for the podcast. Due to our personal interests and ideas, we have long since deviated from the book's arguments and tried to explore our own takes on the phenomenon, though.

Alex: Matt approached me and it just made sense. It's a bottomless well of good topics.

What was the first thing you remember seeing on TV or at the movie theater?

Matt: I think the first movie I saw was either Mary Poppins or Chitty Chitty Bang Bang. This was when Disney would re-release their movies to theaters, or maybe I saw them on TV. I was always more of a reader and my psyche was formed from singing chimney sweeps, flying roadsters, 19th-century classics, David Eddings books, and mid-20th century sci-fi novels. Oh, and Japanese Saturday morning cartoons like Voltron.

Alex: The Greatest American Hero, Electric Company, and crying in the movie theater at E.T. going all chalky and near death.

What performer or artist/writer inspires you the most?

Matt: I've always been most inspired by creators that blend insanity, a wild, untethered imagination and technical prowess. So people like Jimi Hendrix, Hunter S. Thompson and Robert Anton Wilson. If I had to pick one it would be Hunter S. Thompson. I love his ability to blend a fictionalized funhouse narrative with penetrating insight into any real situation. The more I research the Long Seventies though, the more I realize how difficult it is to separate ourselves and our analyses from our circumstances.

Alex: What he said. I'm a big fan of edutainment, hence the podcast. I like nonfiction writers that can spin a good yarn as much as any author.

What other areas of art are you involved in?

Matt: I don't know if it rises to the level of art but I dabble in digital collage work and music. Most of the posters for the show and the intro music are combinations of random or non-random (but symbolically meaningful) photos I pull off the internet and audio samples. I'm no Negativland. I just don't own any instruments, so samples and MIDI are my musical palette. Alex is the show's instrument collector. I use Photoshop for the collages and Reaper for the music and podcast editing.

Alex: I've enjoyed playing and appreciating music for a long time. I'll add experiencing trash cinema to the list, especially since I was scared of horror movies as a kid. I always feel like I have some catching up to do as both a consumer and a creator.

Do you think your environment, where you live, has an effect on type of art you create?

Matt: I think that what defines our environment has changed drastically in the last twenty or so years. The internet has expanded our nervous system to reach across the entire world and connected us psychotronically with people and minds that do not share a physical environment. I think that my environment growing up offline provided a certain stability and taste that informs my research and art, but the internet has expanded my subject matter and memeplex drastically. This hybrid analog/digital environment probably does have a lot to do with what I create because it motivates me to explain the past to people and create a bridge between those two spheres and people who only experienced one of them.

Alex: It goes without saying, but you've got to look beyond the coasts for the interesting stories. I think it pays to be region-neutral in your outlook.

What long term goals do you have?

Matt: I would like to turn the podcast into a series of print books as well as explore what I call "The Other Very, Very Long Seventies" which is the time period from 1870 to 1945. I sense that this period is another historical turning point like the Long Seventies and helps explain much of the world as it stands today. I would also like to appear on Jeopardy, but only if Alex Trebek hosts and the show is Long Seventies-themed.

Alex: Keep on truckin'. But seriously, Matt makes a great point about the late 19th century being a time of fascinating weirdness and variety in its own way. We've talked about a 1990s podcast too.

What do you think the popular culture will be like in ten years?

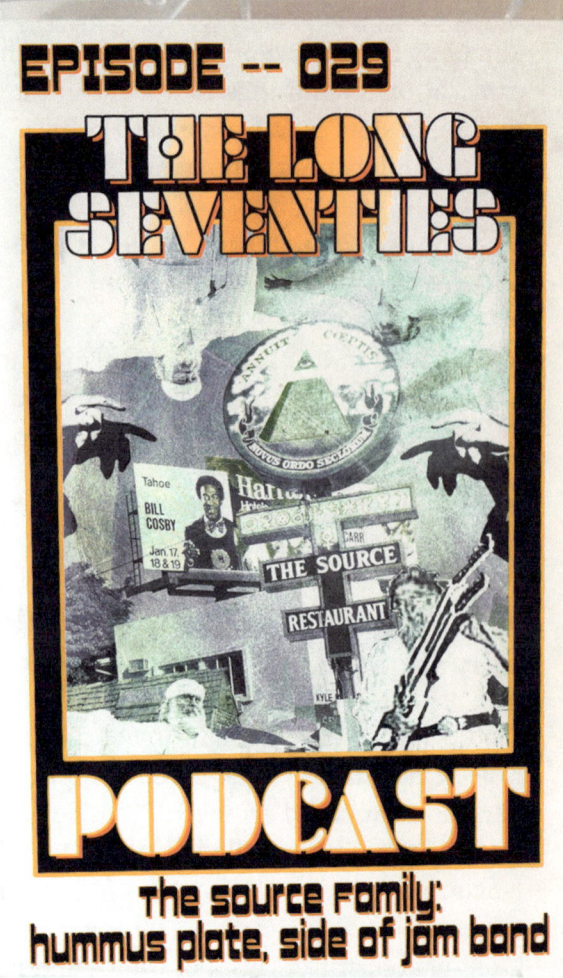

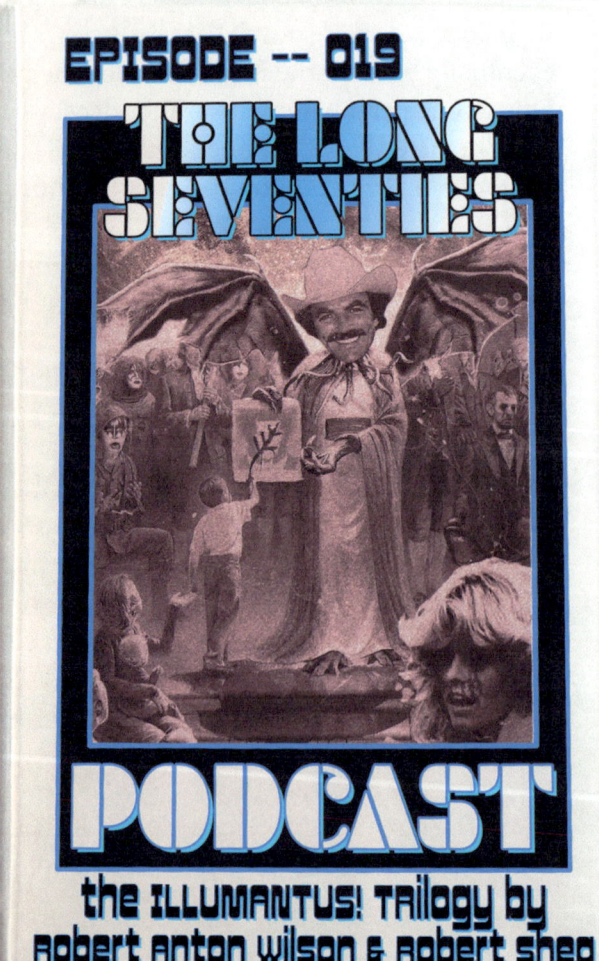

Matt: I don't think Pop Culture has existed for over a decade, and I don't believe it will exist in ten years. Pop Culture was a function of 20th century mass media technology and marketing campaigns aimed broadly at the public in general. Media technology and marketing is now too narrowly focused and tailored to produce any kind of popular consensus reality. Instead we have and will have in the future Schismatic Culture designed to emulate Pop Culture, but restricted to niche interests and often inscrutable to outsiders. The decentralization of culture creation and the internet's disruption of institutional gatekeeping means that attempts to create Pop Culture like Marvel movies and the Game of Thrones franchise (music too) must compete with millions of independent creators that are able to build and maintain audiences much more in tune with their specific tastes and interests. This is why mass media is increasingly hauntological in nature, mining the Pop Culture of the past for nostalgia artifacts they can market to people who consume the past as a series of brands.

Alex: It's really hard to say. On one hand, current pop culture seems hard to relate to a lot of the older pop culture, but the appreciation of retro is strong and people are still finding and making all kinds of art with a foot in the past.

What other things would you like to explore as a podcast?

Matt: The best way to understand the dynamic between Alex and I is to look at us as Rust and Marty from Season One of True Detective. The podcast is our unmarked police car, rolling down the backwoods highways of Louisiana. There is a constant tension between my instinct to investigate hallucinations of Outer Gods and synchromystic alchemical rituals and Alex's relatively anchoring interests in revolutionary communist groups, Afrofuturist musicians and early '80s Peavey guitar amps. This results in a fairly stable and coherent course locking the two together almost like a zipper. Luckily for us the Long Seventies is an almost unimaginably deep well of content to explore, and the deeper into the well we dive the more we find ourselves reevaluating our earlier ideas and connections, which makes the whole experience a constant enrichment. That is probably a long-winded way of saying I have no idea, we make subject choices on the spot based on what we are interested in at the moment.

Alex: Hopefully I won't have to beat the shit out of him in a parking lot. But, yeah, Rust and Marty.

What projects are you working on now?

Matt: I really only have one project, and that is understanding post-1870 U.S. history on a meta level. I won't speak for Alex but what we have been able to understand of this time period has really been due to the two of us applying our precious and limited personal time and attention to the subject over about a four-year period. Neither of us has the benefit of academic sinecure allowing us to devote all our time to history, so it's really been a team effort to overcome the limits of time and space. I expect to continue with this project because at the end of the day it's really about having fun and interesting conversations. We are grateful for our dedicated listeners but I suspect that we'd probably be doing The Long Seventies even if nobody was listening.

Alex: All true. I stumble on topics and find how they lead back to this time period, or I learn of something new and think "Of course that happened in the Long Seventies. We'll have to do an episode on that sometime." We've found with this project that there's always something new to fit into it, or a new take on a familiar topic.

Rising Phoenix

Where are you from? What is your background?

Hi I'm Rising Phoenix a pin/up alternative model, burlesque performer and fire breather. I'm originally from a town near London but brought up and still live in a small rural town in Northamptonshire in the UK. I've been modelling and performing for about 5 years but more seriously for the last year or so.

In the last year I've performed on stage as a solo performer for the first time and as well as in a troupe, it's such a buzz being on stage.

What inspired you to become a model?

I hadn't ever thought of modelling as I actually was really shy, but on a night out I was approached by a photographer (not as dodgy as it sounds) as I was in my usual vintage attire and stood out, he asked if I'd do a shoot with him and that was my first dip into modelling, I then found Jukebox Beauties who are a duo that Mentor and photograph in the vintage theme and it's taken off from there.

What are the pluses and minuses of modeling?

The pluses of modeling are that I get to legitimately show off, seeing the final photographs after a shoot and the work of putting an idea together with the perfect hair and outfit is such a good feeling, it's given me so much confidence not just from any positive reactions but how strong and empowered it has me feeling, as I have said from a shy girl to a strong phoenix. I get to wear amazing outfits, have make up done and work with amazing people.

I honestly can't think of any minuses ,I'm sure there are but they pale into insignificance alongside the good points.

What performer or artist/writer inspires you the most?

The performer that inspires me the most has to be the amazing Dita Von Teese, she is everything I aspire to be, when I grow up I want to be Dita. As a performer she is on point, her look, her stage presence how she moves Dita can do no wrong.

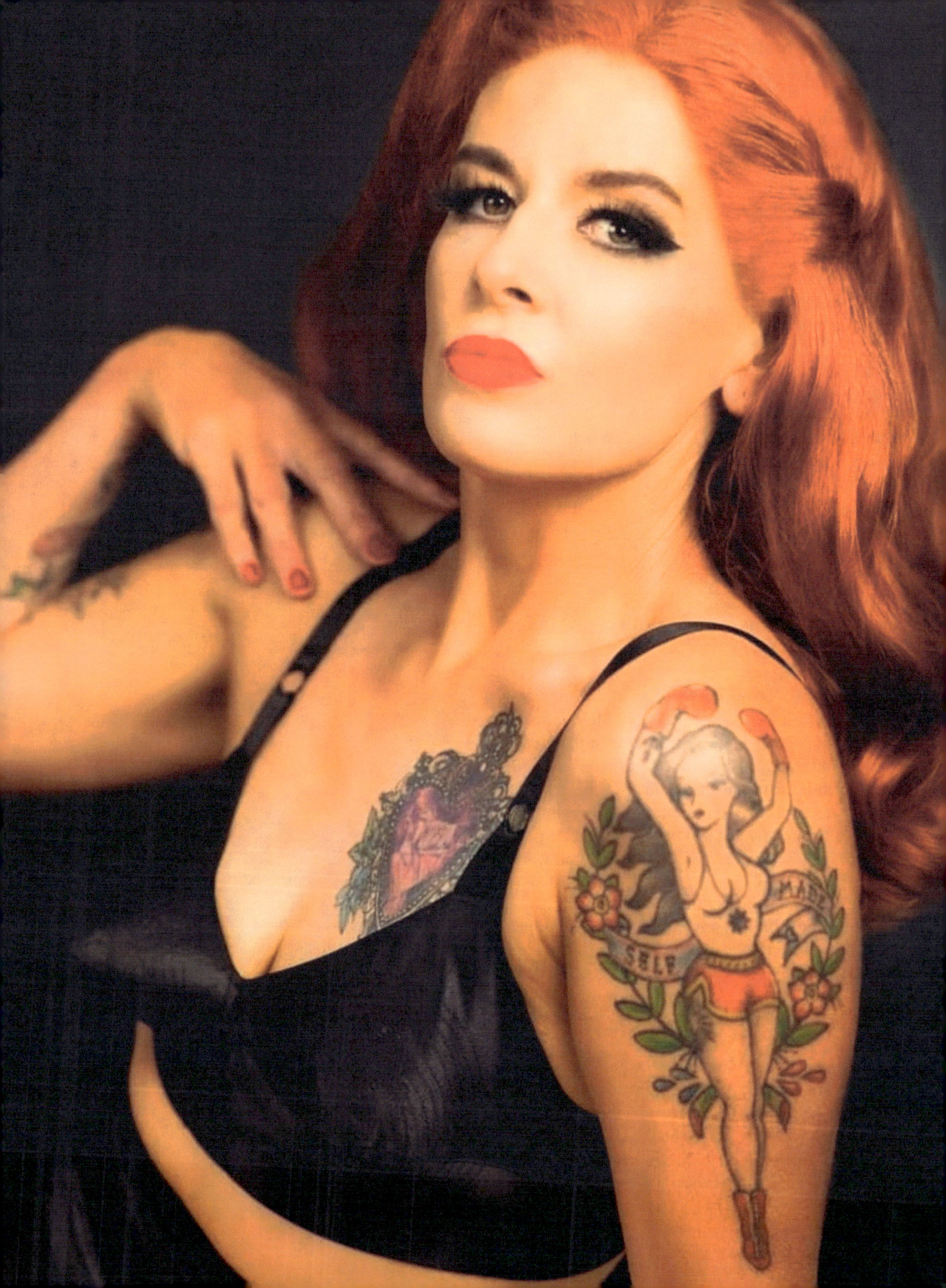
SELF
MADE

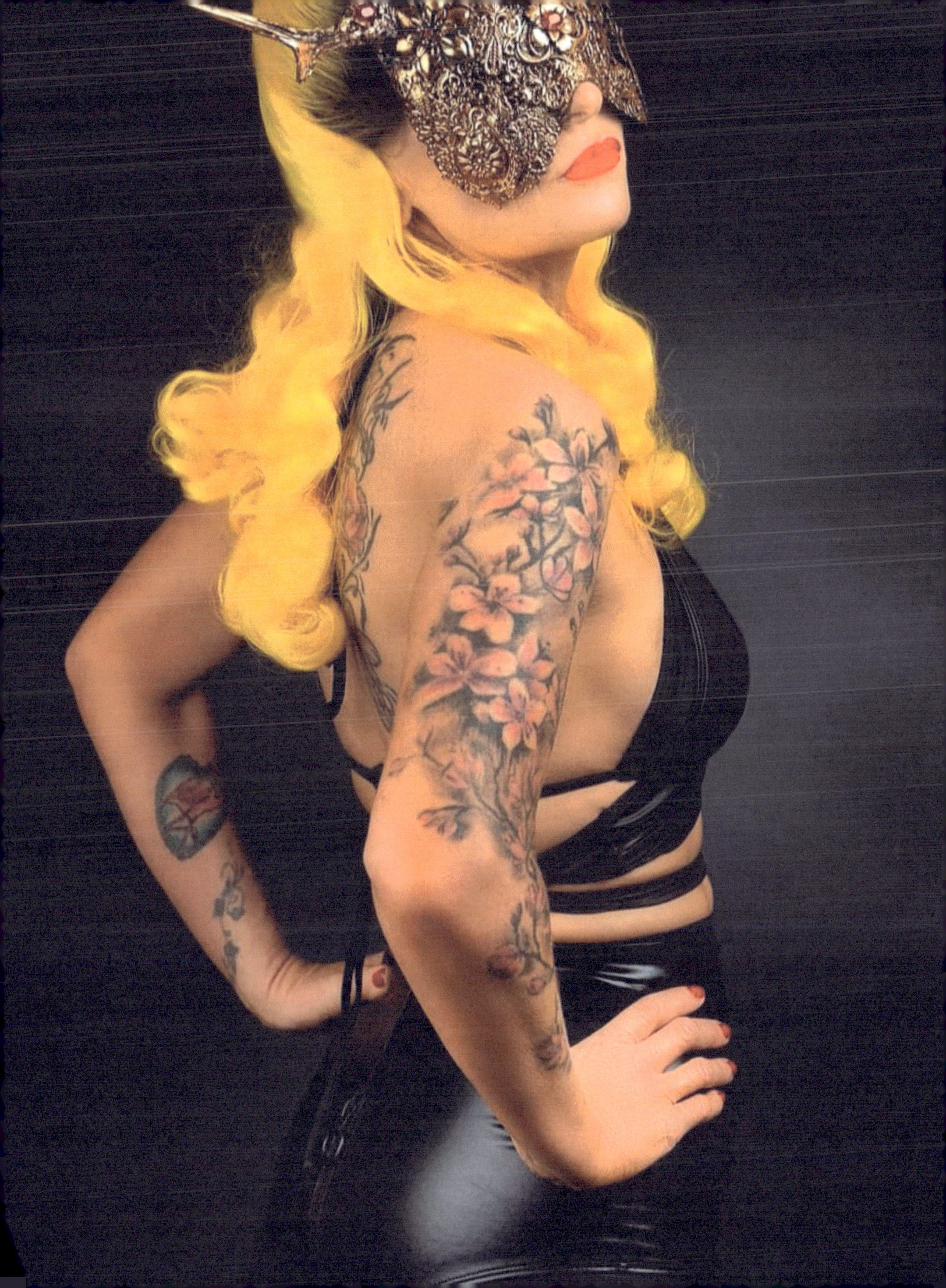

What other areas of art are you involved in?

I also dance in a burlesque troupe and as I solo performer, I have also performed with Fire Body Burning on stage in a burlesque routine.

Performing on stage is something I never imagined I'd do, but there I am throwing my bra off and seductively moving around in front of hopefully a crowd, although one show we had two in the audience (no promotion at the venue).

Before going on, the nerves sometimes get to where I can't remember the moves or what I'm doing but as soon as the music starts a switch is flicked and off I go.

Do you think your environment, where you live, has an effect on type of art you create?

I live in a quiet town where, no offence to anyone, most wear what is deemed as fashionable and a lot dress to conform. I don't and maybe that's part of the reason why I wear vintage clothes and do my best to push away conformity. I've been told its very brave to wear the clothes I do. No I wear what I want as I'm more than okay being me.

What long term goals do you have?

Long term I want to be in more magazines, be on the covers of magazines, travel further afield to shoot and keep on trying different styles. I of course want to be performing more and at bigger venues.

What do you think the popular culture will be like in ten years?

The way popular culture will be in ten years hopefully will be with women being able to have the freedom to express themselves with their own bodies without being censored, I have had two photographs banned on Instagram that showed the top of my bottom that was covered with sheer fabric! I really hope the future has us having permission to show the human form, in obviously a classy way—my body my choice not a censor deciding for me.

What's the strangest thing thing you've been asked to do in your profession?

I've only had one strange request and that was one I didn't take up, was to photograph my feet, I run to keep fit so my feet aren't something anyone really wants or needs to see, so for all concerned I declined that request

What projects are you working on now?

Coming up I have a burlesque show and I have 5 shoots over the next month coning up which I'm really excited about, shooting in latex, as a Viking warrior, a vampire, a sexy Winifred Sanderson (something I don't think any would expect), and a recreation of The Kiss in Times Square.

And of course working with Twisted Pulp magazine.

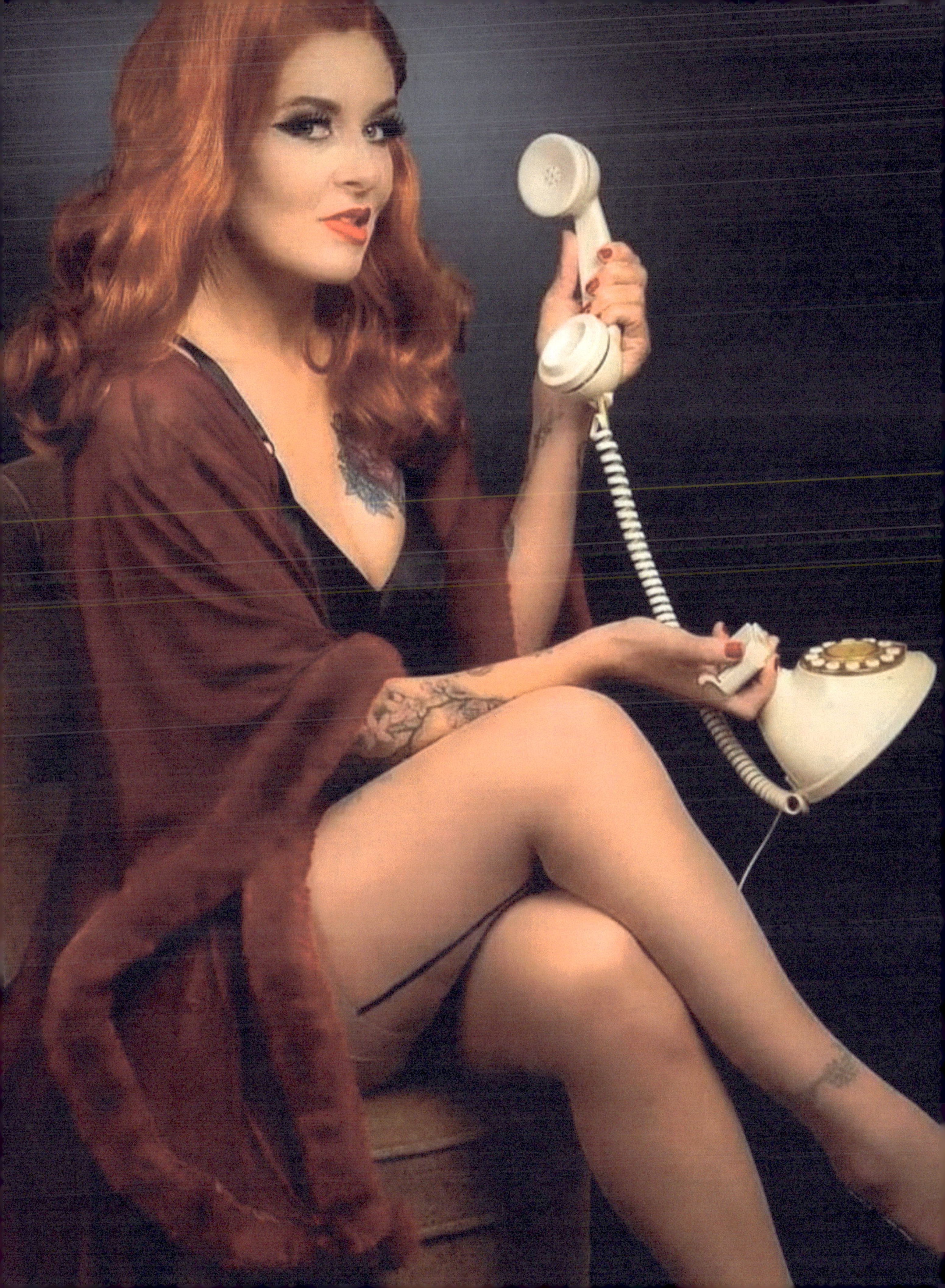

COSPLAY CORNER WITH AMANDA

In our last column we covered basic tools needed for basic cosplay techniques, so in this issue's column we will cover how to use certain tools for more advanced techniques. Techniques such as heat shaping with tools like heat guns, ovens and soldering irons to manipulate working mediums such as Worbla (also known as thermoplastic which there are different varieties of) and a rotary tool like a Dremel for shaping and shaving foam and other materials.

Heat shaping can be used to manipulate and modify many different cosplay and crafting materials such as thermoplastics, foam, and styrene. Thermoplastics need heat to activate them, by using a heat gun you can quickly and evenly heat a sheet of the thermoplastic for sculpting and for use in molds. Worbla is a brand of thermoplastic that has several varieties available, brown worbla is good for armor bases and big builds that need surface area coverage as well as small detailing. Black worbla is very smooth and used for pieces needing a smooth finish like a prop sword or prop gun. Worbla also has a clear and pearlescent option for glass and gemstone look-alikes. Once heated Worbla and other thermoplastics become malleable, though very hot to handle so gloves are recommended when sculpting. As thermoplastics cool they harden into the shape, if you need to reform a piece all you need to do is reheat it!

When using heat to form foam, the thickness of the foam and the shape of the piece need to be considered before heating. Foam comes in many different thicknesses and the thinner the foam the less time heating needed, and always keep in mind that foam can burn if heated too long with a heat gun! Shape comes into play when heat shaping in regards to curves and sharp angles. When heat shaping foam into curves for things such as female breast plates a form is needed to either heat the foam directly on or to pull the foam onto to shape it. For sharp angles cuts are made on the opposite side of the foam to facilitate a nice clean edge.

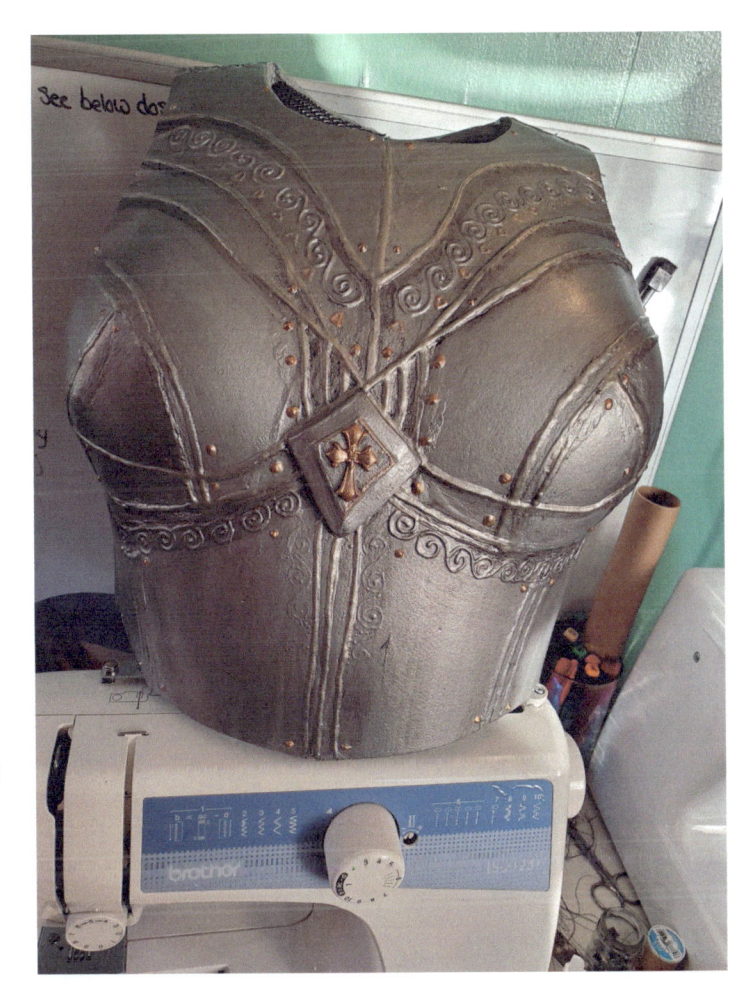

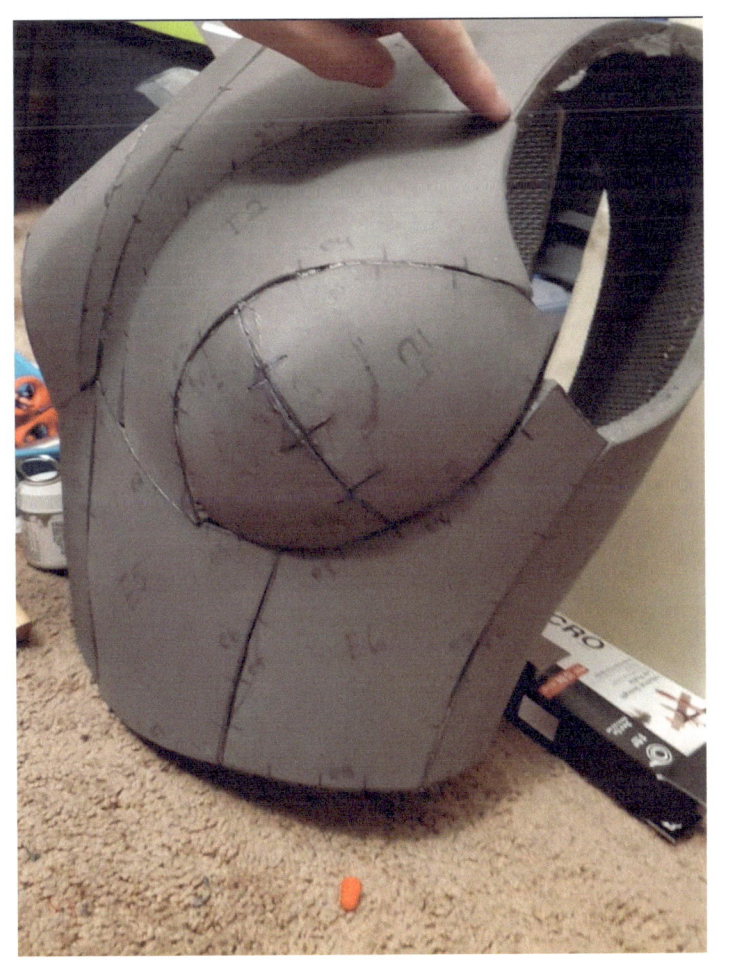

Some materials like styrene have a super low melting point and using the right PPE (personal protective equipment) like goggles and a respirator, you can use heat to create battle damage and melting effects for props and set items. A soldering iron can be used to create detail damage in thermoplastics, foam, and styrene since it can be used more precisely. Soldering irons can even be used to help trace details into cooled worbla and poking uniform holes through foam! With all the materials easily available online or even in most craft stores, getting started with worbla and foam is super easy and there's a tutorial for every technique! As always safety first! Feel free to reach out and ask questions over on my Instagram @ladydevinecosplay !

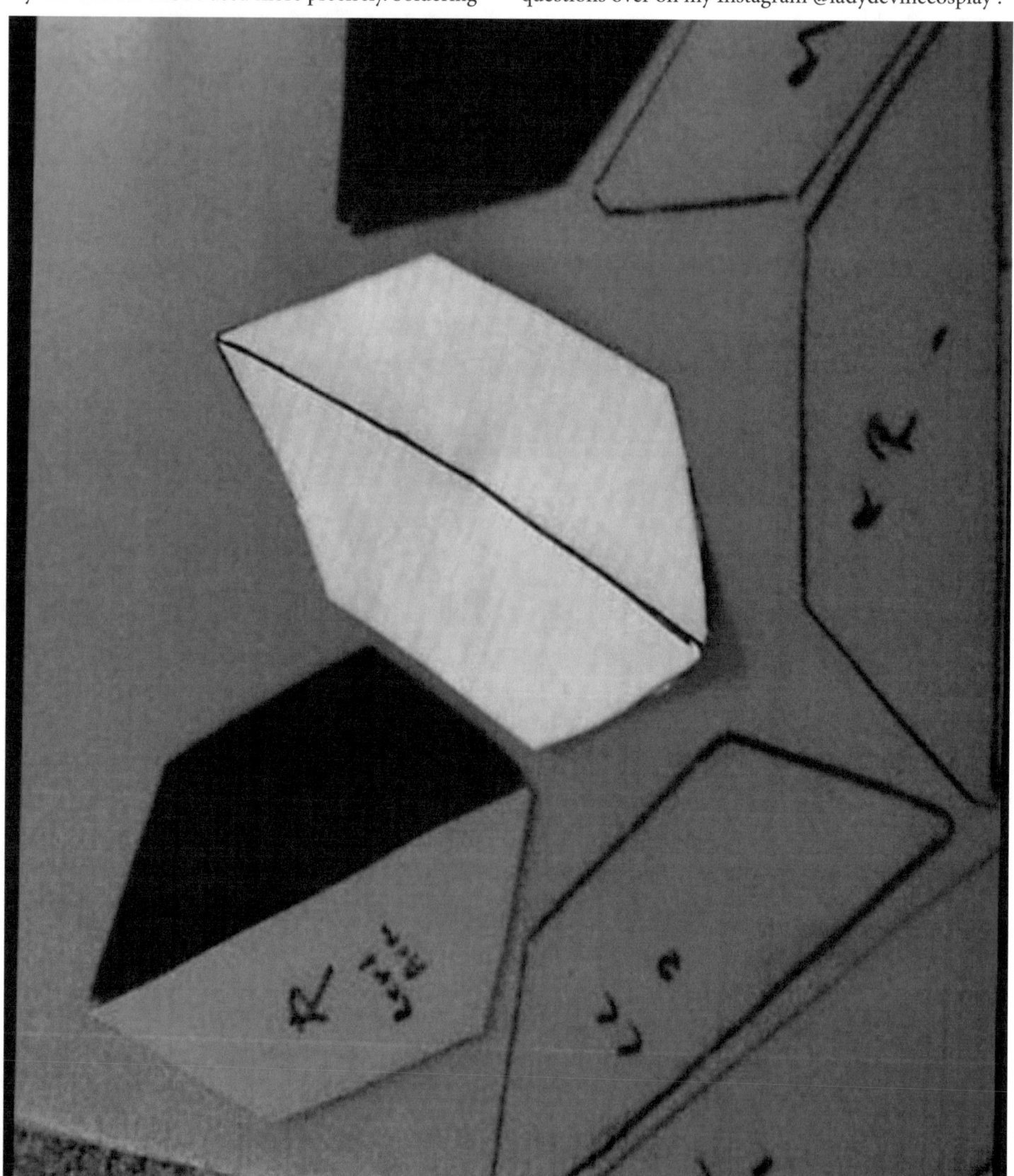

SERMON INTERRUPTED

BY MARK SLADE

Sermon Interrupted

By Mark Slade

John was supposed to be writing his sermon, but with sex on his mind it was too hard to concentrate. The TV was too loud as usual, a girl squealing, nonsense chattering, voices blaring. I was in the kitchen washing the dishes. John was in the living room watching one of his movies when the doorbell rang. He hit pause on the remote, listened.

I poked my head in the living room to listen, as well. The doorbell rang again, a constant church rattling, one right after the other. The person at the door didn't even have the common decency to let the call resonate before pushing the button again.

"Are you going to get it?" John asked, the remote still in his hand, glass of bourbon in the other.

"Well, dear," I told him, "Since you are in the living room and I am in the kitchen, I think I'll let you get it. How's the sermon coming along?"

John rose from his seat, which still retained that new-chair squeak whenever anyone stirred, six months after Sadie and Billy gifted it to him for Christmas. How those two scraped up enough money to buy it, I'll never know, both of them still in college.

John placed his glass on the coffee table but not on coaster, as usual. After twenty-two years of marriage, training that man was near impossible.

"Yes, dear, I shall get the door," John said. "I'm not doing anything but writing the Lord's word for a weekly get together."

"Rubbish," I told him. "You're sitting in front of the TV getting sloshed. Now answer the door, John Carson."

I hung around the kitchen threshold, wiping down a bowl over and over, curious to see who was at the door at seven p.m. on a Saturday. Most people in town were in their own homes watching TV or tending to their families or finishing a game of golf.

The bell chimed again.

"I'm coming, I'm coming," he bellowed, shuffling toward the door. He opened it quickly.

Nora Simmons stood in the doorway, wearing her skirt too short, her cleavage too revealing. Nora was one of those sorts who always clung to another woman's man a little too long, the kind who would sit in the front row, crossing and re-crossing her legs, talking a bit too close to them, letting her hand linger on a gentleman's knee or shoulder.

John shuffled his feet, and began stuttering, swallowing after every sentence. "Oh, hello, Nora. Kay? Look who it is," John called out to me. "It's Nora, darling."

"I can see who it is," I said, wiping down that bowl even harder, faster.

"Gracious," Nora said, her smile as plastic as her personality, as phony as her dyed red hair. "Can I come in or am I interrupting a romantic interlude between you two?" She stepped inside, not waiting for an answer, her jutting breasts brushing past John. He coughed, sniffed, made a false gesture to show her the way.

"What brings you here, Nora?" John fiddled with his glasses, then returned to his chair, sheepishly trying to avoid looking as Nora's skirt rode up slightly when she sat on the couch across from him.

"I need to speak to you and Kay. It's really important." She made a dramatic pause afterwards, pouted. "Kay?" she called out to me. "Can I speak to you in here? This concerns you as well."

Reluctantly, I joined them in the living room, and sat beside her, feigning a smile. I even touched her knee, thoughtfully. "What's on your mind, dear?"

"It's a delicate matter." Nora flashed a strained smile. "You realize that Tom and I are getting a divorce. He has good lawyers, and… I have George." George was her brother.

George was a simpleton and a terrible lawyer even when he's sober.

"Something happened four months ago, Kay. I'm not proud of it." Nora turned to John, gave him a cool look, reached into her handbag and produced a DVD with no label. "I'm sure…" She looked back at me, bit her lower lip. "You'll hate me for this. I know you will, Kay.

John and I, while it was fun, Tom had this crazy idea of filming us."

John looked ahead, eyes transfixed on nothing in particular. He looked a little white, sickly. Nora continued. "I myself was not going to do anything but watch it once in a while. It's us in living color, Kay. John… and I. The truth is… if I don't get twenty-five thousand dollars, I might feel compelled to tell the congregation. Maybe the news people, too? I just need enough money to get to Tampa Bay, start over… I've met someone."

The room fell completely silent, the air thick with tension. I stood suddenly. I didn't say a word. I went to the closet, opened the door. I touched my handbag, the red Carmichael, the one John had gotten me on our wedding anniversary.

Nora's face brightened up. "Oh, thank you, Kay!" Her voice went up in pitch, into the decimal range only dogs could hear. She turned to John. "Don't feel bad, John, dear, think of it as giving to someone much poorer than you."

The baseball bat came down hard on the base of Nora's skull. It felt weightless in my hands. The old Louisville slugger belonged to Billy when he played in high school. I kept the bat tucked in the closet behind my handbags for just such occasions. I swung again, this time the sound more wetness than crack. I swung once more, and the blood splattered the couch like an abstract painting. Nora had slouched over to the left, the back of her head flattened.

"Well?" I said.

"I need to finish my sermon."

I stared until my gaze burned a hole through the back of his head.

"I mean, I'll finish the sermon later tonight," he said automatically.

"Damn right." I dried my hands. "Now drag that whore around back with the others."

Katiya Rose

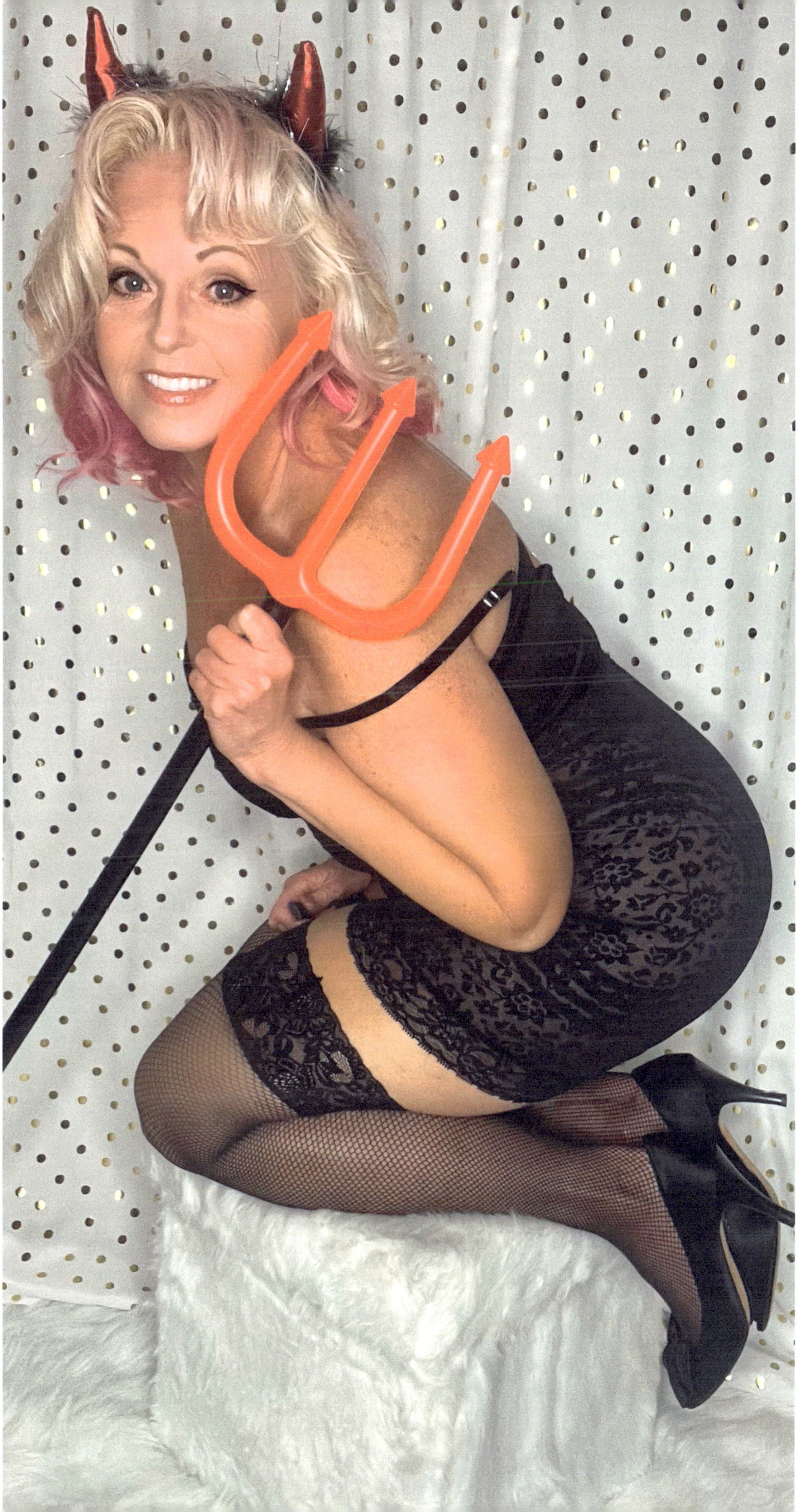
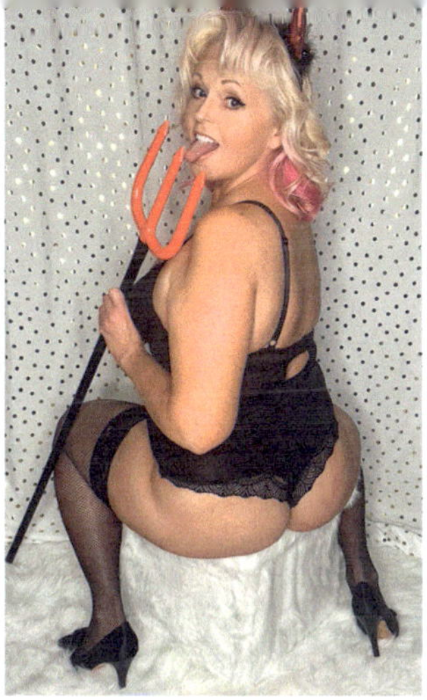
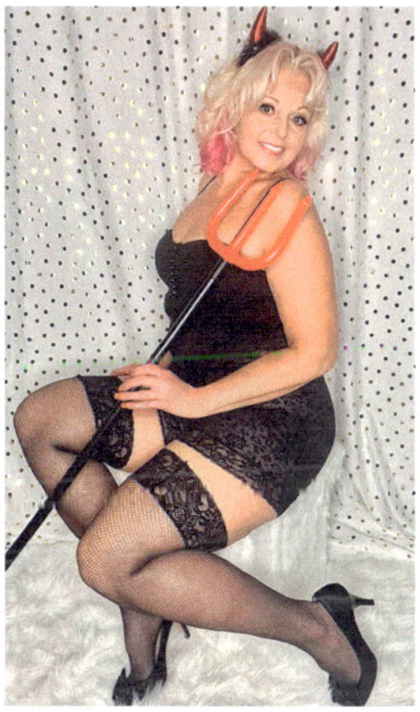
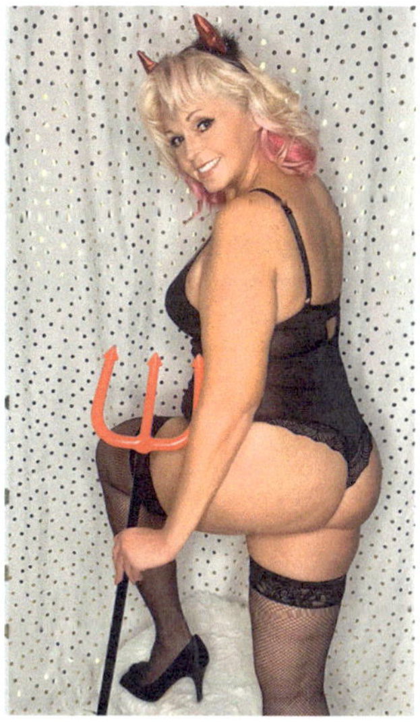
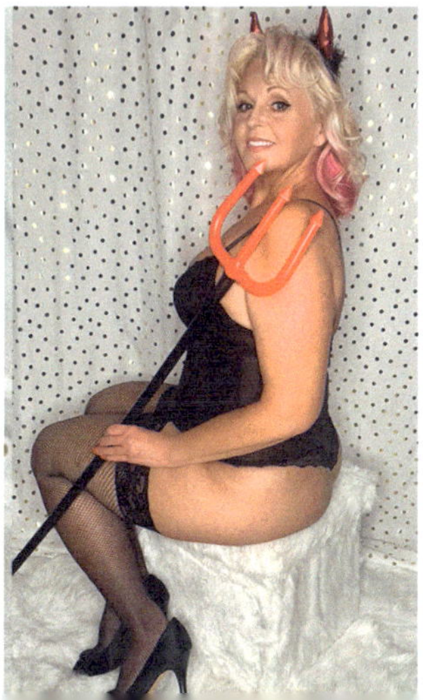

Where are you from? What is your background?

Born and raised Texas girl. I was a tomboy growing up, climbing trees and making mud pies in the pretty dresses Momma put on me. I live on a farm, and raised goats and two daughters. After they were adults I went back to work outside the farm and ended up becoming a cake decorator.

What inspired you to become a model?

I've always loved vintage pin up art. My favorite pin up was Duane Bryers' "Hilda." She was a country girl like me, and always up to something. I was diagnosed with multiple heart conditions ten years ago and really let myself go. After finding the right cardiologist, things turned around and I lost over 40 pounds and regained a lot of my confidence. My youngest daughter "dared" me to post some pics on Instagram. That was in February this year and its been a wild ride! I found out I really enjoy the whole creative process of it. I do all of it myself, sourcing vintage slips and furs, hair, makeup, and taking the pictures. The feedback and support has blown me away, and I'm so thankful.

What are the pluses and minuses of modeling?

Pluses, it keeps me mindful and taking care of my physical well being. I meet a lot of cool people online, and hopefully brighten their day a little. I get to play dress up for hours! Minuses, I do get occasional negative feedback and told to "act my age." But I remind myself I have yet to come across a manual outlining what I can and cannot do at any given age, so I continue to happily do what I want.

What performer or artist/writer inspires you the most?

"Bunnie XO." Besides being gorgeous, she seems like a genuinely sweet, caring woman. She doesn't sugarcoat things, and you never know what she's going to do next. And she's a great example of not letting a dark past keep you from a bright future.

5. What other areas of art are you involved in?

Cake decorating. Unfortunately I'm on hiatus from that due to some issues with wrist pain. I also sew, and used to sell "upcycled" clothing on Ebay. I also collect antiques and vintage items, I love incorporating them into my backdrops.

Do you think your environment, where you live, has an effect on type of art you create?

Yes, its pretty quiet and peaceful out in the country. It helps reduce my stress after work and resets me. Trees, sunsets, whippoorwills at night, the smell of rain in the summer. Although if I lived in the city, I would probably have way more access and time to thrift more vintage stuff!

What long term goals do you have?

I would like to keep improving my pin up art, get a real camera, better lighting. I hope to keep doing this for a while. I'm about to turn 53, so I kinda got a late start at it. It's a good reminder to be thankful for every day I'm above ground and not below.

What do you think the popular culture will be like in ten years?

I think things will turn more nostalgic. We're already seeing a little bit of a turn towards this with social media. So many of the younger generation are getting into thrifting, antiques, crafting and discovering movies and music from the past.

What's the strangest thing thing you've been asked to do in your profession?

I've been asked to make some pretty strange, and at times, inappropriate cakes. The most memorable one was a tiny 1/8 sheet cake, frosted in light pink, blue trim, with daisies, and written on it "Death Is Closer Than Ever." Young girl in her 20s picks it up, it was an online order, I didn't take it in person. I asked her the story behind it, she said it was a birthday cake for her Mom. Apparently Mom must have a good sense of humor. I've also put an edible image of a pinup photo of myself on a cake for a coworkers brother as a surprise. He LOVED it!

What projects are you working on now?

Working on some ideas for Christmas theme photos. I have some sewing projects upcycling some damaged vintage slips and fur.

63

CHAPTER TWO "THE CLOSING TRAP"

As darkness descends on Lisbon, the lights of the Cafe Estrella beam down on a dancer... her breathtaking beauty quickly draws Portuguese phrases of praise from the local customers...

"AMOR, VANIDA!"

"BEBEREMOS A VANIDA!"

And outside, a native guide tries to draw the more profitable tourist trade...

"WANDER ABOUT NO MORE, SENHORES, SENHORAS...THE CAFE OF YOUR DREAMS EES HERE! ENTRAR, ENTRAR!"

"OH-OH, THAT PORTUGUESE PITCHMAN'S PUTTING THE FINGER ON ME NOW!"

"YOU, SENHOR, YOU LOOK LIKE A JUDGE OF BEAUTY! LOOK HERE AT OUR MENINA VANIDA!"

"YEAH, SHE'S THE GIRL OF MY DREAMS, ALL RIGHT! CHUBBY, YOU'VE JUST CAUGHT YOURSELF A CUSTOMER!"

"A TABLE, SENHOR?"

"FIND ME A CORNER SPOT—AWAY FROM ALL THE HULLABALOO!"

"YOU WEESH TO ORDER, SENHOR? VINHO, PERHAPS?"

"VANIDA, PERHAPS...HOW'S FOR GETTING HER OVER HERE AFTER SHE FINISHES THAT FANDANGO?"

"THAT EES EEMPOSSIBLE, SENHOR! EET EES AGAINST THE RULES AND..."

"...AND IT'LL TAKE ABOUT TEN ESCUDOS TO CRACK THE CAFE'S CONSTITUTION, RIGHT?"

Minutes Later

"OH!"

"THAT 'OH' SOUNDS LIKE THE START OF A DULL CONVERSATION! BETTER LET ME TRY TO SNAP UP THE DIALOGUE!"

"FOR A STARTER, LET ME SAY THE 'FIVE FINGERS OF SATAN' DATA IS OLD LACE TO ME! YOU AND LATHAM OVERLOOKED A CARBON COPY LEFT BY MURAT!"

"SECONDLY, I'M GOING TO BREAK THOSE FIVE FINGERS—ONE BY ONE—UNTIL I REACH THE UNHOLY HAND THAT MAKES YOU DIGITS DANCE LIKE PUPPETS!"

"BY 'BREAKING,' I PRESUME YOU MEAN TO BETRAY ME TO THE LOCAL POLICIA?"

"UH-HUH—JUST AS SOON AS YOU LEAD ME TO YOUR SIDEKICK—LATHAM!"

As Latham tightens the trigger, Vanida tenses and allows her eyes to drift toward the gun...

"OH-OH, THIS GAL'S GONE AND GOTTEN HERSELF A NEW LOOK! SOMETHING'S GOING ON BEHIND ME!"

"BETTER DIVE FIRST AND LOOK LATER!"

BAM!

"LATHAM—NO—UGH!"

65

VA-VANIDA... I DIDN'T MEAN... VANIDA!
I'LL TAKE THE GUN, PAL!
PAULO! COME! TROUBLE EES BACK THERE!
THE DANCING GIRL...S-SHE EES DEAD!
HOLD IT, HAMLET — YOU'RE TACKLING THE WRONG VILLAIN!
DON'T MOVE, SENHOR!
THE MENACE IN THIS ONE-ACT DRAMA IS...OH-OH! LATHAM'S BOWED OUT OF THE SHOW!
WITH LIGHTNING SPEED, DICK GRABS THE CANDLE BOTTLE...
HATE TO BREAK UP THE SHOW SO SOON, CHUM, BUT THIS IS MY CUE TO STAGE A FAST EXIT!
BAM
HEADWAITERING IN THAT SMOKY DIVE MUST HAVE RUINED THAT GUY'S GUN-EYE!
AVOIDING THE POLICE-PATROLED PORTUGUESE STREETS, POWELL FINDS "LODGING" IN A LOCAL PARK...
BY MORNING, LATHAM SHOULD BE MAKING HIS NEXT MOVE... AND I'VE A FAIRLY GOOD IDEA WHAT IT'LL BE!
11

67

Panel 1: MIDNIGHT, ON THE MEDITERRANEAN, FINDS THE FREIGHTER FIGHTING A HEAVY SEA...

Panel 2: TOSSING AROUND IN THIS TWO-BY-FOUR CABIN IS GETTING ME DOWN! THINK I'LL GRAB A BREATH OF FRESH AIR!

Panel 3: LOOKS LIKE THE DECK'S DESERTED! GUESS THE REST OF MY SHIPMATES ARE EITHER IN THE THROES OF SEASICKNESS OR SLUMBERING!

Panel 4: NOT QUITE ALL OF THEM, DICK...! POWELL!

Panel 5: HMM..THIS LIFEBOAT'S BUCKING LIKE A BRONCO! BETTER LASH ITS DAVIT BEFORE IT DIVES OVERBOARD!

Panel 6: HERE'S THE PERFECT SITUATION — PLANTED RIGHT IN YOUR LAP, LATHAM! THE TIME, THE PLACE... AND THE **WEAPON!**

Panel 7: CAN'T SEEM TO GET IT! GUESS I'VE SORT OF FORGOTTEN MY "HALF HITCH AND SQUARE KNOT" SCOUTING DAYS!

WHEW! THAT LAST BREEZE BLEW A BLAST OF PIPE ASHES INTO MY EYES!
MAYBE I'D JUST BETTER FORGET— LATHAM!
YOU'RE AWFULLY ANXIOUS TO SPLIT UP OUR ACQUAINTANCESHIP, AREN'T YOU?
OKAY, PAL, I'VE GOT AN AXE TO GRIND, TOO ... AMERICAN STYLE!
UH-H...
SMAK
HERE'S ONE FOR THE SAPPING YOU GAVE ME IN JAN MURAT'S APARTMENT...
AND HERE'S FOR THE LITTLE FRACAS AT THE CAFE ESTRELLA!
JUST AS POWELL'S BLOW LANDS, THE SHIP ROLLS VIOLENTLY TO ONE SIDE...
LOOK OUT!
AAAAGGHHHHH
14

"A TOUGH WAY TO GO— BUT BETTER HE THAN I! BETTER NOTIFY THE SKIPPER!" / As if soothed by the death of Latham, the sea calms and the balance of the voyage to Athens is a pleasant one...	"GOTTA MAKE READY TO RUN INTO MENACE NUMBER THREE... THE TALL THIN GREEK CALLED PETROS! HE'S PROBABLY PERCHED ON THE PIER, WAITING FOR LATHAM!"
"THAT LANK COULD BE THE LAD I'M AFTER...CAN'T BE SURE, THOUGH! WISE THING TO DO IS KEEP MY EYES OPEN AND MOUTH SHUT!"	After the Acantha's passengers are all ashore, the tall man makes an anxious query... "EXCUSE, PLEASE! THERE WAS NO MR. LATHAM ABOARD?" / "YEP...THAT'S PETROS!"
"I'M MOST SORRY TO SAY, SIR, THAT MR. LATHAM MET WITH A FATAL SHIPBOARD ACCIDENT!" / "LATHAM..DEAD ..DEAD? AND A MR. POWELL ...WAS THERE A MR. POWELL?"	"YES, THERE WAS, BUT I PRESUME HE'S GONE ASHORE!" / "LATHAM MUST'VE WIRED PETROS ABOUT ME, BEFORE HE BOARDED THE ACANTHA AT LISBON!... OH-OH-HE'S SHOVING OFF NOW!"

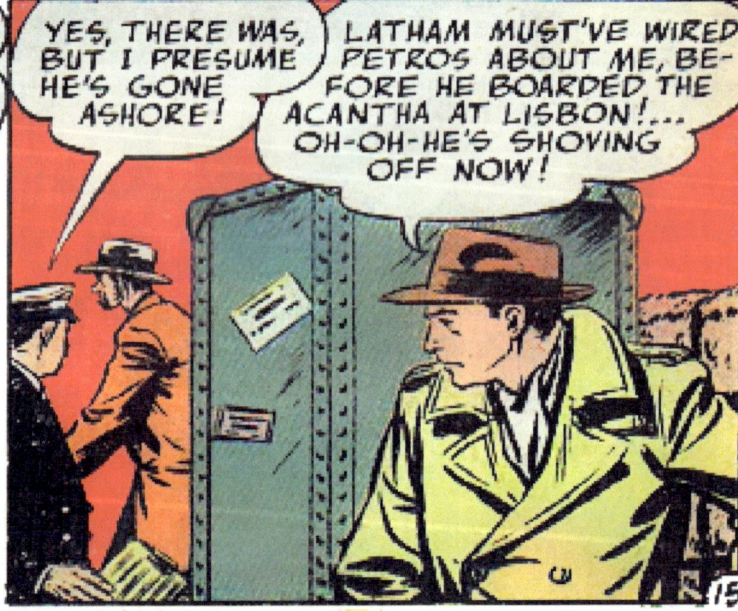

PICKING UP THE TRAIL, POWELL PURSUES PETROS ALONG THE WINDING WATERFRONT STREETS.. FINALLY...

HE'S DUCKING INTO A TELEGRAPH OFFICE! NOW THE TRICK IS TO FIND OUT JUST WHAT HE'S SENDING TO WHOM!

THIS MESSAGE WILL BE SENT AT ONCE, BOY?

YES, EFFENDI! AH-EXCUSE ME A MOMENT!

MAY I HELP YOU, EFFENDI?

NOT AT THE MOMENT, THANKS! JUST WANTED TO GLANCE THROUGH THESE TRAVEL FOLDERS!

GOOD... HE DID HIS SCRIBBLING ON A PAD! SHOULD BE ABLE TO PICK UP A FAIR IMPRESSION OF THE MESSAGE FROM THE SECOND SHEET!

BOY!

THERE HE GOES! THIS SPY CHORE IS GOING SMOOTH AS SILK... ALMOST TOO SMOOTH!

BUT PETROS GOES ONLY AS FAR AS THE OUTSIDE TELEGRAPH OFFICE WINDOW...

SOMETHING ABOUT THAT MAN IS NOT RIGHT...SOMETHING! AH-HAH! HE TEARS A PAPER FROM THE TELEGRAPH PAD!

PETROS, YOU ARE PLAGUED WITH A MOUSE-LIKE MEMORY! OF COURSE ...HE IS THE ONE WHO DESCENDED THE GANGPLANK AT THE DOCKS!

71

72

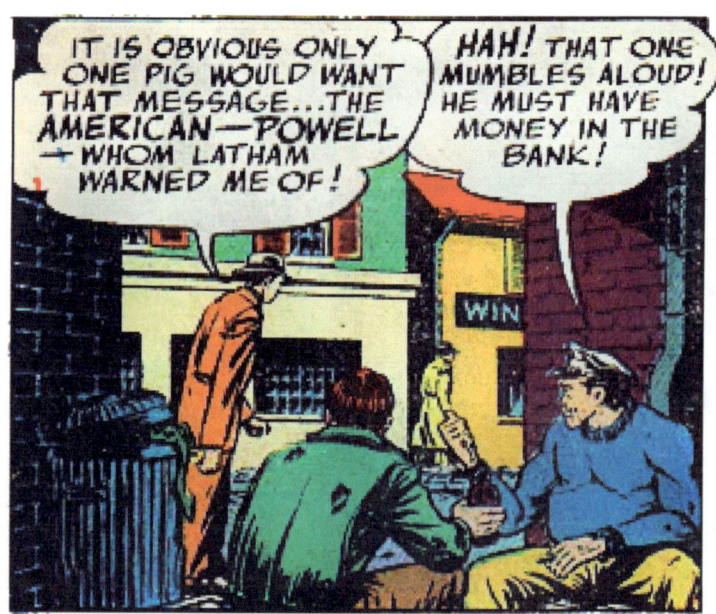

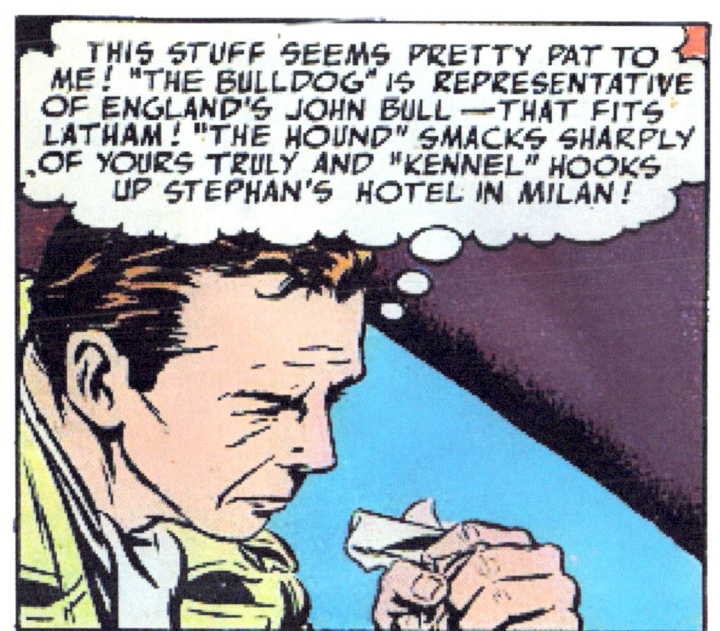

THIS STUFF SEEMS PRETTY PAT TO ME! "THE BULLDOG" IS REPRESENTATIVE OF ENGLAND'S JOHN BULL—THAT FITS LATHAM! "THE HOUND" SMACKS SHARPLY OF YOURS TRULY AND "KENNEL" HOOKS UP STEPHAN'S HOTEL IN MILAN!

WITH ALL THAT INFO, I SHOULDN'T HAVE MUCH TROUBLE TRACKING DOWN—OH-OH! DID I SAY TROUBLE?

COME, WHY DO WE WAIT?

THERE ARE OTHERS IN THERE, IMBECILE! A DISTURBANCE WILL BRING THE POLICE! PATIENCE WILL BRING HIM OUT TO US!

AND.. A HALF HOUR LATER...

I'VE CHECKED THIS BEANERY FROM STEM TO STERN AND THERE'S ONLY ONE EXIT... THROUGH THAT DOOR. AND IF I DON'T GO OUT THEY'LL COME IN—AS SOON AS THIS LUNCH CROWD LEAVES!

LEONIDAS, LOOK!...ACROSS THE STREET!

PAH, WHAT IS THERE TO WORRY? HOW COULD OUR PRISONER AND THE POLICE GET TOGETHER, WITH US STANDING HERE?

POWELL, WHO HAS ALSO CAUGHT SIGHT OF THE OFFICERS, PONDERS THE SAME QUESTION...

WAIT A MINUTE, I'VE STILL GOT ONE STRAW TO CLUTCH...THOSE COPS ACROSS THE STREET! I HATE TO DO THIS, BUT—!

NO, EFFENDI! I BEG OF YOU...NO!!

18

TWISTED PULP
MAGAZINE

Made in the USA
Columbia, SC
22 March 2024